Praise for
Women Who Knew The Mortal Messiah

*"I loved it. One of the most tender and uplifting books
I've ever read! I highly recommend this book
for every Christian woman!"*
—Anita Stansfield, Bestselling Author
Romances with a Real-Life Edge

*"Reading these tender stories strengthened my faith in Jesus
Christ. It's a book filled with hope, love of the Savior for
all, and a certainty that He lives."*
Kristin Holt, Author

*"I love this book. I have read all the stories many times and
always feel the Spirit when I do."*
Marie Barnhurst

*"I had a hard time putting this book down! A word of
warning--keep the Kleenexes close by!"*
Diane Stoddard, Author

"These stories took me on a sacred journey."
September Hullinger

*"I absolutely loved this book. Reading it took me back to
the Holy Land of long ago. A great read."*
Valerie Steimle, Author

Books by Heather Horrocks

Women Who Knew The Mortal Messiah

Upcoming Releases

A Visit With Three Women Who Knew
Musical Program

You Just Turned 8
A Baptism Book for Children--And Their Parents!

Women Who Knew The Pre-Mortal Messiah

MEN WHO KNEW
The Mortal Messiah

SPECIAL FIRST EDITION

Welcome to the special first edition of my new book, *MEN WHO KNEW THE MORTAL MESSIAH*.

This is the companion volume to *Women Who Knew The Mortal Messiah*, released in March 2004. The series will continue in 2006, going further back in time into the pages of the Old Testament with *Women Who Knew The Pre-Mortal Messiah*.

You are one of a limited number of people to receive this special first edition. I hope as you read that you feel closer to your Savior and His healing Atonement.

May we also know . . . *as long as there is a Savior, there is hope*.

Heather Horrocks

MEN WHO KNEW
The Mortal Messiah

Heather Horrocks

Word Garden Press
P.O. Box 27208
SLC, UT 84127-0208

www.menwhoknew.com

ISBN 0-9748098-1-0
Printed in the United States of America
Alexander's Digital Printing, Lindon, Utah

Available at bookstores and online.
For personalized autographed copies, go to
www.heatherhorrocks.com.
For wholesale bookstore orders, call Deseret Book Distribution at 1-800-453-3876.

WORD GARDEN PRESS
P.O. BOX 27208
SALT LAKE CITY, UTAH 84127-0208

SPECIAL FIRST EDITION June 2005
10 9 8 7 6 5 4 3 2 1

Cover Photograph Courtesy of Charles Escue © 2005

Inside Sketches Courtesy of Barbara Benson © 2005

Dedicated to
all God's children
who seek
to know Christ.

Also to those of God's children
who are also my children.
I hope you will always seek
to know Jesus, your Savior.

ACKNOWLEDGMENTS

I thank my Heavenly Father. This book, from beginning to end, has been a walk in faith for me. My hope is that this book be pleasing to my Lord.

Thanks to my readers, who have responded so positively to both *Women Who Knew The Mortal Messiah* and this volume.

I would like to extend my appreciation to Charles Escue for the use of his beautiful photograph of the vine and grapes used on the cover. Thanks for your generosity.

Thanks to my talented cousin, Barbara Benson, for the delightful grape and vine sketches that add so much to the inside pages.

This section wouldn't be complete without talking about Diane Stoddard and Kristin Holt, two of the most awesome critique partners ever. Thanks for telling me when it works--and when it doesn't--and for all the support you provide me. It's always good to have the Motivation Monitor and Punctuation Police on my side.

Thanks to my "cold readers" (Sylvia Jones, Kathleen Wright, Ken and Pam Benson, Mark Horrocks) for your help in making those final changes that add so much.

Thanks also to my friend Allen Richardson and to Nelson T. Dinerstein, for answering the scriptural questions put to you with such knowledge.

Thanks to my wonderful son, Patrick Fenn, for helping me with the technical side of things.

Thanks to Kristeen Polhamus, for composing the beautiful music of the song *There Is Hope* for my musical program, *A Visit With Three Women Who Knew*.

Thanks to my sisters, September and Skye, for always being there for me, no matter what.

Thanks to my father, Reid Hullinger, for finding the silver lining behind every hardship.

And thanks to you, Mark, for walking beside me on the journey. It is so much better with you here by my side.

TABLE OF CONTENTS

PREFACE

I am the vine, ye are the branches:
He that abideth in me, and I in him,
the same bringeth forth much fruit:
for without me ye can do nothing.
(John 15:5)

Wherefore by their fruits ye shall know them.
(Matthew 7:20)

These stories are of actual men who lived on the Earth during the Savior's life and ministry, some Apostles, others disciples, all flawed in their humanity.

I have worked to keep the stories scripturally and historically accurate. They have been fictionalized, as some scriptural references are only a few sentences long, one merely implied (Joseph). This is my interpretation.

I have presented these thirteen stories of these twelve men in chronological order, so the entire book would be a picture of Christ's life and earthly ministry, from beginning to end, as seen through the eyes of these men. These stories are designed to fit naturally with those contained within *Women Who Knew The Mortal Messiah* and, to help with reading them together, I've included a chronological list at the end of the book.

Please know that if you find anything of beauty in these pages, it comes from our Heavenly Father.

Though these men lived two thousand years ago, Jesus still lives today. Christ's power to heal is as great now as if He still walked the earth, as though He placed His hands upon our brow and blessed us Himself, as if He looked into our eyes, as if He said, "Follow me." We can be healed as surely as if we sat blind before Him on the path, as surely as though we could not walk but had to be lowered through a roof before Him, as surely as though we brought our child to Him.

We may know others by their fruits. Christ's ministry and Atonement has brought about the greatest and sweetest harvest ever. His apostles also bore fruit of sweetness and light. What is our fruit?

Through Christ, we can be born again. From darkness into the blessed light of Christ. *Alleluia!* For unto us is born this night a Savior. The star still shines. Wise men and women still seek Him. The light still heals. The harvest still grows.

I pray again that the spirit and light of Christ may touch our hearts. That our testimonies, our witnesses of Christ, may grow stronger each day until they fill our hearts and souls. That we may become men and women who *know*--as long as there is a Savior, there is hope.

Men Who Knew
The Mortal Messiah

When Herod the king
had heard these things,
he was troubled,
and all Jerusalem with him.

(Matthew 2:3)

CHILD OF THE STAR
Wise Man

"He is an evil toad," spits out Melchoir to break the long silence. We have traveled half the night, far from Jerusalem, but Melchoir wisely does not say the name aloud. We will not know if we have been followed until our servants return.

I cannot but agree with my friend. Herod may be King, but he is indeed an odious man. And we have experience to judge such a thing. for we have just been forced to waste a sennight at the palace. Seven days we have wasted.

My camel steps into a low spot and I grab the side of the lurching saddle. When the road levels off, we return to swaying back and forth. I have ridden ships of the sea, and it is much the same. And I have grown used to the sensation, as we have traveled for over a year, joining with large caravans for safety.

1

Holy men in our own country, we searched the sky diligently for the sign, for we knew the time was nigh and we were prepared. Our journey began with that glorious night when the new star appeared dramatically, a brilliant point of light like a diamond set on a background of richly textured black cloth, announcing that the Messiah indeed had been born upon the earth.

We know enough astronomy that we recognized the new star. Surprisingly, not all did, and fewer saw its significance, though it has been prophesied for generations that a new star would point the way. As soon as we saw the sign of the true King, we completed our provisions and said our farewells.

Not a mere tetarch appointed by the Romans, such as the arrogant Herod, but *The King*. The awaited one. The Messiah. Immanuel.

The holy Child of the Star is born, and we seek Him.

I left my country also for another reason. My dear wife of thirty-seven years left this earth and the pain of her loss still clenches my heart. I hoped that time away would ease the ache, but a year of bouncing on camels and thinking of her has only made her loss more intense.

We have followed the star from our own country, traveling ever westward across a major trade route, until finally, north and west of the sea of salt, we turned southward.

When we reached Jerusalem, we knew we were close. We inquired of the people, saying, "Where is He that is born King of the Jews? For we have seen His star in the east, and are come to worship Him." To our astonishment, instead of rejoicing, they grew troubled at our words. Perplexed. All of Jerusalem!

We wondered at this. What has happened to the people of Jerusalem that they know not their King is born? Why would the knowledge of their Messiah's birth cause them such concern? How could they, of all people, miss the sign?

King Herod also became troubled when our words were carried to the palace, though he feigned otherwise. Immediately he issued an invitation for us to join him at a private banquet. Tales of Herod, a man so evil and brutal that he murdered his wife and several of his own sons as well as many of the Sanhedrin, had even traveled to our county, far to the east. Thus we dared not refuse.

Herod spoke with us privately, asking the first of many questions, and then sent us to feast while he met with his advisers. This we learned by asking of the servants bringing food, who were amazed to be spoken to with courtesy.

After Herod met with his advisers and we ate, he called us back, again privily, to his rooms of state, where he was alone once again with only a trusted servant to bring him wine in a gold cup--a gold cup we presented to him to show respect for a king whom we do *not* respect.

In answer to our question--*Where is He that is born King of the Jews?*--Herod told us of a prophecy quoted by his chief priests and scribes. "Thus it was written by the prophet: *And thou Bethlehem, in the land of Juda, art not the least among the princes of Juda; for out of thee shall come a Governor that shall rule my people Israel."*

Bethlehem! The child was born in Bethlehem!

Excitement coursed through my veins--*We are so close!*--until Herod with his words dispelled it. He said the skies had become cloudy and the star could not be seen, and so he insisted we tarry with him. Though we were anxious to press on, both to find the child and to be free of Herod's evil presence, again we felt we must do the king's bidding.

That night of clouds stretched to seven.

Usually even my dreams are filled with my wife and thus my loss each morning begins anew. But the first night at the palace, I had a different, vivid dream, being warned of God that we should not return to Herod after finding the child, whose face I saw. When I awoke, I whispered my story to my two friends, and discovered, to our amazement, that they also had the same dream.

Thus we will depart for our own country another way, along one of the three routes south from Jerusalem, down to Beersheba and east around the southern edge of the Dead Sea--but this new plan we have kept between the three of us, Melchoir, Gaspar, and myself, Balthazar. We have not shared it even with our trusted servants. When we speak of our journey home, it is always as though we will retrace our steps to Jerusalem and from there go north and then east toward our home.

While we tarried with Herod, we answered his many, many questions. *How long ago did the star appear? Have you spoken with any who have seen the child? Where did you gain your information of the star?*

Realizing Herod's desire to harm the child, we pretended to be such fools as to be flattered by the attention of a king, as to be honored to return to Jerusalem in another fortnight to tell him where we found the child. Never has such a thing been more difficult for me than to pretend to admire King Herod!

But thus we did pretend, and reassured him because we refuse to lead a jealous and brutal Herod to the Child of the Star. It was imperative we convince him, else he would send spies to follow us, and that must not happen. The child must be kept safe at all cost, even if that price includes our lives, if need be, for we have put the child at risk by bringing Him to Herod's attention.

Thus we smiled and left gifts and flattered the odious king. And when we readied ourselves to proceed south, Herod smiled falsely and enquired diligently for the young child, "And when ye have found him, bring me word again, that I may come and worship him also."

I snort in disgust at the memory. "He does not mean to worship the child. Did you see how troubled he was with the thought that there was a king of the Jews born who had been prophesied for generations?"

No, whatever Herod has in mind for the Child of the Star, it is certainly not worship. We knew that within minutes of meeting the false king, even before the dream of warning. We suspected when he met with

5

us each time separately from his advisers, whom we never met during the sennight. Apparently Herod wanted no one to know of his evil plans for the true King.

One would have to be a fool not to realize Herod never made mention of the child when anyone else besides us was present--and we are not fools.

I am thankful this night that we have God on our side, to warn us of Herod's duplicity, to guide us in our words and actions, to help us be better pretenders than the evil king.

At sunset, under the light of the moon and the new star, and with great relief, we left the palace.

And with even greater relief, I now catch sight of the two trusted servants we instructed to linger behind our main group to watch for spies. If they are here, it means Herod has sent no one after us. And indeed our men report that none follow us. We have escaped Herod with our lives and thus with the life of the child.

And, lo, halfway through the night, the Star of the King, which we saw first in the east and which has gone before us nearly four hundred days, now stands over the place of the child. And we know we have arrived at our destination--the place upon which the star shines.

We halt our camels and stare, awestruck, rejoicing with exceeding great joy.

The star has led us to a small house in the village of Bethlehem. The star seems to shine right onto this dwelling, alone. How that is possible, I know not, but I know that with God all things are possible--even a star pointing to one house among many.

I clamber down from the saddle to the earth, hand the reins to my servant and take a few steps to become re-accustomed to the ground no longer swaying beneath me.

There are two hours before sunrise, and we will wait until morning before disturbing the people of the household, though it will be hard to wait. Yet what are a few hours when we have already traveled so far?

We use the time to prepare ourselves, pitching our tents, cleansing ourselves, dressing in our finest robes.

As I sit, sipping tea, the old familiar pain still throbs in my heart. In only a few hours, we will meet the promised Messiah. My dear wife looked forward to this day also, but was taken from me before the sign appeared.

We send the servants away to rest for awhile but we do not desire sleep. Instead we sip our tea and reminisce, speaking freely between us as we could not in the palace.

We speak of the star, the caravans, and our long journey to find the Messiah Child.

We prepare our gifts. Melchoir's gold rests heavy in its secured chest. Gaspar's frankincense, a rare gum resin used as a base for sweet fragrances. My myrrh, prized as a perfume and unguent used in embalming.

The value of these gifts is enormous. We are holy men, but that does not mean we are without wealth. Also we represent others who could not come, and they have generously given gold with which to honor the new King of the Jews.

We did feel led to leave a few of the lesser pieces of gold with Herod, even the cup, to convince him of our sincerity. But we hid the rest, the best, under guard, keeping it safe for the Child of the Star.

Light begins to creep through the edges of the tent, and still we wait. One hour more that moves more slowly than any before.

Morning sounds begin to filter through our tent. A cock crows. Sheep begin to bleat. A cart rumbles past.

Finally, it is time. Gaspar offers a prayer of thanksgiving that we will soon be in the presence of the new King. My heart quickens within my breast.

I stand to adjust my robes, then lift my small ornate chest containing jars of myrrh. When I glance at my companions, I can tell they share my deep feelings. We stand, savoring this moment of joy and awe and wonder, for there will never be another like it.

Another King will never come, for this King will be forever King of the Jews. Forever Messiah. Forever Immanuel.

Finally, I draw in a slow, deep breath, soaking in the moment, sealing it in my mind and heart, then I smile with joy and say, "Let us go and worship the child."

We three go to wake the servants to help carry the weight of the gold we bring, only to discover they also have been too excited to sleep.

We stride from our tents and across the path to the house, dressed in our best, ready to honor the King.

A large man with muscled forearms and strong hands stands at the door of the house, as if guarding the way from those in our caravan. He is cautious, as well he should be, if he knows anything of Herod's jealousy. I see character and kindness in the man's face. A strength of more than body alone. It would be wise if a guard was also kept at night.

After Melchoir explains why we are come, the man nods in recognition and relaxes. He knows the child of whom we speak and is not surprised to have strangers seeking the child to worship Him.

The man introduces himself as Joseph, the carpenter, originally of Nazareth, and says he is the husband of the child's mother and thus the child's caretaker. I am pleased to observe the task rests on such responsible and capable shoulders.

Joseph invites us into his home and bids us place our chests in the corner.

In surprise, we see that the dwelling is quite plain. Not so grand as our homes in the east, but nice enough. There is a scent of freshly cut wood in the air and finely crafted furniture worked from rich wood.

Joseph introduces us to his wife, Mary, a startlingly beautiful young woman, most fair and delightsome to look upon.

This radiant maiden is the mother of the King, and we give her due honor and respect. When she is assured of who we are and of our intent, she steps aside. I see a child peek from behind her skirts.

I recognize His face from my dream!

9

The Messiah!

I am overcome with emotion. As the holy spirit of God whispers that this tiny child is indeed the promised Messiah, I fall on my knees before Him.

Mary tells us, "He is called Jesus, as the angel instructed."

He toddles around His mother and stares at us. He is young, barely over a year, for this is how long since His star appeared.

He is the age of my smallest grandchild.

A year of riding upon camels, swaying back and forth and thinking and praying and meditating upon the new King--and here He stands before us. He is but a mere babe, still unsteady on His feet, but I can see the light of His countenance, even at this tender age. My heart tightens within my chest and, for the first time in years, tears come to my eyes.

Melchoir and Gaspar prostrate themselves beside me, our servants behind us, and we pay homage to our King.

I feel a tiny hand on my arm and warmth spreads through me. The babe touches my face, smiles and speaks in the babbling way of babies before they can be understood. But I sense He knows what He says and what He does. I understand that the child Jesus, young as He is, wants me to rise, so I lift myself onto my knees.

When the child looks into my eyes, I gasp at the power and the love that emanates from this mere babe.

And I am loosed from my pain. I see with great clarity and what I see is my wife and I, safe and reunited.

As the vision fades, joy fills my heart. I *will* be with my wife again. We will be together throughout the eternities. For this purpose has the child come--to reunite us all with our Father which art in heaven.

He touches each of us in turn, and the sound of our sniffling fills the air. We cry as though we are the children. My heart burns within me and my soul sings with joy and thanksgiving.

After we have composed ourselves and wiped our tears of joy, we present our gifts.

The babe laughs aloud, and the delightful childish sound of it brings joy that I cannot measure.

My heart lifts within my breast. The memory of our days with this child will light the many days of travel which await us. This will be a year of thanksgiving as we return to our own country and our homes and our families with the good news.

I would like to return to see Him as He grows to manhood, but I am aged now. This glimpse of the promise is enough for my lifetime.

Though I know we must shorten our stay and be gone long before Herod realizes we do not plan to return, I will savor forever my few glorious days with the Child of the Star.

Jesus, the Savior, is here!

Immanuel! God is indeed with us!

The King is born! Forever may He reign!

And when they saw Him,
they were amazed:
And His Mother said unto Him,
'Son, why hast thou thus
dealt with us?
Behold, *thy father* and I have
sought thee sorrowing.'

And Jesus said unto them,
'How is it that ye sought me?
Wist ye not that I must be
about *my Father's* business?'

(Luke 2:48-49)

A FATHER'S FOOTPRINTS

Joseph, Husband of Mary

I am not so old to be unwell, yet neither am I well. I have kept going through my days, despite the pain, but this past fortnight it will no longer be ignored. Those years when I could move easily, with great strength, are past. All my life, I have been blessed with a strong, healthy body. Without thought, I hefted wood of all sizes and shapes, planed it to size, chiseled, hammered, joined, and smoothed, all tasks requiring physical strength. Now it is too much effort to move, even slowly, and so I have taken to my bed.

My sick bed.

My death bed.

I know it is time for me to leave this earth. My family does not accept it, but as the Lord wills. I admit I am ready to go.

I hear my beautiful wife, Mary, in the kitchen, fixing delicacies to entice me back to health. She feeds me well, as one does a babe, hoping to bring strength back into my limbs and color into my cheeks. I force myself, for her, but I have no appetite, and indeed I can eat little despite my best efforts to please her. And I have always wanted to please her, my beautiful Mary, since I first saw her.

My children have come to visit with me. Indeed someone has been with me most of the time, and I can see by the sadness in their eyes how far I have faded from my once vigorous self.

But for this quiet moment, I am alone and thus there is time to think. More and more, my thoughts have turned to my life and the accounting I will make to my God.

When He asks what I have done with the gifts He has given me, with His charge to me, what will be my reply?

He gave me a gift of working wood, and I have used that gift and magnified it and worked wood well. I love woods of all sorts. Cedar. Oak. Ebony. Olive wood. Poplar. Willow. Plane. Tamarisk. Sycamore. Elm. Beech. Acacia. Terebinth for special purposes. I have coaxed them into different shapes and sizes--door frames, cupboards, plates for eating, fancy boxes for holding special treasures, tables and chairs, buildings. I have been the carpenter in Nazareth for many years. Whenever people had need of a carpenter, they would come to me, and I could create whatever they wanted.

None of what I have made is more cherished by me than the dove I have carved these past weeks as my final gift to my dear wife. Groaning with the pain of even simple small movements, I attempt to smooth the still slightly rough surface of the finished carving, but I have insufficient strength. With a deep sigh, I stop rubbing and hold the tiny bird in my hand. It is good, I think, and she will be pleased. At the thought of her, I smile. I chose fragrant cedar from Lebanon for this, my final work, both for its softness to work in my weakness and for the aroma that Mary prefers.

The dearest gift my Father has given me is my beautiful wife, Mary, and I have cherished her always. She is indeed my greatest treasure. My only regret is that when I go I will leave her behind, alone, but that is no longer in my hands, but in His. I have to trust that God will watch over her. I know Jesus will.

Ahh, Jesus. My son--and yet truly not my son.

Most incredible of all, God gave me *His* Son as a babe. Many times have I pondered this blessing, truly the greatest honor any man could ever have. And with this honor came a heavy responsibility, and now a fear that I have not measured up to the greatest challenge ever issued me.

For God did not set His feet upon the earth to leave the footprints for His Son to follow, but He put me here to place those footprints in His stead.

I have tried in all my life to walk in our Father's footsteps--and that became more important when I had a tiny one toddling along behind me. I have never overcome the enormity of this responsibility--to protect and guide the Son of God until He could be led by His Father, and then to step aside and let Him guide me.

As I have listened to Jesus, I know He speaks His Father's truths and His Father's messages--and I can only hope there is a small echo of myself in His words, as well.

Have I done well? I hope I have been adequate, but will His Father agree?

He has certainly been the finest son I could ever have hoped for.

Most amazing of all is the fact that this son of mine, whom I love with all my heart, is also my Savior. Just as Mary has pondered all this in her heart, I do not fully understand what this means, but I know, without doubt, who Jesus is. He is the Messiah, prophesied by Isaiah and Abraham and Moses and all the prophets back even to Adam. He is watched over by angels of the Lord. This I know, for they have spoken with me over the years, and I remember both the messages and the messengers vividly, for their words changed my life.

I still remember my amazement at the dream, or vision, I had, wherein an angel told me, "Joseph, thou son of David, fear not to take unto thee Mary thy wife; for that which is conceived in her is of the Holy Ghost. And she shall bring forth a Son, and thou shalt call His name Jesus, meaning Jehovah is Salvation: for He shall save His people from their sin." And I gladly did take unto me my beautiful Mary, as the angel bade me.

I was no less amazed when, on the very night the wise men pointed their camels back toward their homes in the East, the angel returned to warn me, "Arise, and take the young child and His mother, and flee into Egypt, and be thou there until I bring thee word: for Herod will seek the young child to destroy Him." And I arose before morning to do as I was bid, using the gifts the wise men brought to pay for our sojourn.

And when the angel returned to bring me word that it was safe to take the young child and His mother back to the land of my fathers, again I did as I was bid. Herod's murder of the babes in search of Jesus has haunted me. I am so thankful for His safety, but at such a heavy cost. The land still cries out with their blood.

That was many years ago, and since then I have watched Jesus grow from grace to grace, intelligence to intelligence, youth to man. He treats His mother with respect, and I have taught Him that, I suppose. He works wood as a master craftsman, and I have also taught Him that skill. He treats others with compassion and I taught Him that, as well.

But oh how much more has He taught me, all these years. Mercy. Meekness enough to be teachable, even I who at first taught Him. Companionship. Love. Service. Other than His mother, I have been privileged to be in His presence for more hours than any on this earth as we spent hour after hour, year after year, working side by side in the carpentry shop.

I have listened to His words--from His very first, which were Mama and Dada. Though I am only His father by proxy, yet I live the role and I cherish the word. And I have listened to many other words from Him through the years--amazing words. He understands all--and is gentle with mine own lack of understanding.

And when I have doubted my abilities, I have relied on God's trust in me.

He is God's beloved Son, for thus the Holy Spirit as a Dove did announce when Elisabeth's son John baptized Him in the River Jordan. And He is also Mary's beloved son, for I have seen her great love for Him. And I love Him as a father loves his son--and also as a son of God loves his Savior.

As if my thoughts have summoned Him--something that has happened many times before--I hear Jesus calling out as He always does when He enters our home. *Peace be unto you.*

Calm fills my heart. Jesus always carries peace with Him and I draw strength from Him now, in my weakest moments. I take comfort in knowing Jesus will care for His mother when I am gone.

I know He will care for her even when He begins His ministry. He has not said, but I have seen the signs in Him. He has changed, somehow, as though it is time to put off the mantle of His mortality and put on the mantle of the Master. It is truly His time now to be about His Father's business. Even at the age of twelve, when it was not yet His time, He amazed the priests in the temple. Now He will astound the world.

I see the light in Him, the majesty, the purity and strength. I see Him preparing for His life's work even as I slow to the end of my own, struggling this day even for breath.

As Jesus enters the room where I am laid, His smile is sweet, but I see the concern on His brow. I know He has been comforting His mother, who grieves my leaving.

And I *am* going. This I sense. I feel my strength fading, as though I am a leaky vessel.

Jesus touches my cold, clenched hand with His warm one. "What is this?"

I reveal the carved dove. "It is for your mother. I have shaped it but have not strength enough to smooth it."

He lifts the bird from my open hand and inspects it in the morning light from the window, nodding in approval as He turns it this way and that. "It is good. She will be pleased."

Now our roles are reversed. Jesus is the able carpenter and I the unable one. He the teacher, I the student. He the caretaker, I the cared for. He the Father, I the son. Now I know how my gift will be completed. "Will you smooth it for me?"

He nods and sets the dove carefully on the table by my bed. "First let Mother see your work of love, then will I smooth the wood."

Now Jesus places His hands upon my head to bless me. I feel the power in His hands and I know He can make me well, if it is God's will for me. His words this day, for me, however, are not words of renewal, but of comfort and love. Thus I truly know it is my time to go, and my heart is calm and the pain subsides somewhat.

And perhaps it is only fitting that it is now my time to go. The Jews are waiting for a Messiah to lead them. They want a King who will throw off the yoke of the Roman conquerors. I am in the lineage of the royal family. Thus if the Romans were not conquerors, I would be, in fact, the King of the Jews. At one time, in my youth, the Jews hoped it would be I to lead the rebellion against the Romans, but this has never been my task. Neither do I believe it is the task of Jesus. No, His work is much larger still. Thus the Jews will be disappointed still. But it is only because they do not understand.

With my death, Jesus will take my place in the royal line descended from David the Shepherd King. The world believes Jesus is the son of my loins, and He is in truth Mary's Son, and she is also of the House of David.

Even without the lineage, Jesus would still be King. The true King. The Prince of Peace.

The Jews are searching for a different sort of king.

I see the pattern and the purpose, both in my place in the royal line and in my death at this time. Everything is as it should be, but that is hard for the others to see. The ones who love me. Those precious to me.

Mary comes into the room and clings to Jesus's arm. Her face is pale and streaked with tears, and I am saddened at her pain.

"Am I so near to death then?" I ask and even I can scarce hear my words, hoarse and croaking and feeble.

Mary, my beloved Mary, sheds tears for me. She touches my arm and says, "I have sent for the others."

I see tears roll down Jesus's cheeks, as well.

The two people in my life who mean the most to me--my beloved wife and my beloved son--each take one of my hands in their own. I feel love flowing from each of them, but the love from my son is so great it fills my entire body.

"My father," He says, "watch for me on the other side."

"I will be there, my son." Weakly, I voice my apprehension. "If God finds me worthy."

Jesus smiles gently. "I find you worthy, and likewise our Father finds you worthy. You have fulfilled your mission upon this earth. You have been a good and faithful servant." His fingers touch my cheek. "And a beloved father to me here. Go in peace, my beloved father and my dear friend."

Mary's hold tightens on my other hand, but I cannot see her through my tears.

Jesus presses his face to mine and kisses my cheek. "I love thee."

"And I thee," I reply. It is hard to draw breath to speak the words. My little strength fades and flickers as a candle flame in a light breeze.

"Go in peace." Jesus says softly as He pulls back.

Mary leans over me and her tears fall upon my arm. "Oh, Joseph, my dear Joseph. I will miss thee so."

I hear others in the room. More of my children come, even as I fade too far to see.

The next instant there is a brilliant light, bright as the noon-day sun, filling the room with warmth and love, moving outward until there are no walls.

My body still lies abed, but I do not. I slip free, whole and healthy once more, moving without effort or pain, seeing with such clarity I am astounded.

I see them all in my room, my beloved Mary and my children, sorrowing for my loss, yet I sense they will be well. And Jesus, from whom the magnificent light flows, looks at me now, across the veil the others cannot see, and smiles. "Go in peace," He repeats softly.

My Son is shining brightly. My son. Mary's son. God's Son. My Lord and Savior.

Angels are singing praises to the Lord.

I also sing.

23

He drove them all
out of the temple,
and the sheep, and the oxen;
and poured out
the changers' money,
and overthrew the tables.

(John 2:15)

TAKE THESE THINGS HENCE
Seller of Doves in the Temple

It is the custom for each male in Israel to pay an offering to the temple during the Passover, the eight days celebrating the time when the Lord protected and freed our ancestors enslaved in Egypt.

The first offering was a one-time payment made during the building of the tabernacle in the desert. Now it has become an annual tribute, the equivalent of two day's wages for one such as myself.

I am a seller of turtledoves in the temple. If you want pure, unblemished doves for your offerings, you have come to the right place.

Each day save the Sabbath I pull my cart loaded with cages into the shade of the arched colonnades around the eastern edge of the outer court, known as Solomon's Porch, and set up shop.

Though the spring weather of the month of the Abib is cool, it is still too warm for my birds to be in the sun. I learned the care of birds from my father, who sold doves in the temple before me. It is he who taught me love for the winged ones and for what they symbolize, which is the return of the Messiah. Did not Malachi write that *the Sun of righteousness shall arise with healing in His wings?*

The first House of the Lord, Solomon's Temple, was destroyed by Nebuchadnezzer six hundred years ago, and rebuilt five-hundred-and-fifty years ago as the Second Temple. Forty-six years ago, Herod, old rascal that he is, determined to rebuild the Second Temple to the magnificence of the first, and I believe he has exceeded his goal. Indeed, it has been said that he who has not seen the temple of Herod has never in his life seen a beautiful building. Yet still Herod is not done-- after fifty years, the extensive renovations continue. I have never known the temple without construction.

Except Passover week. In honor of the celebration each year, the construction is halted. Though the work chants and bickering of the laborers and the ringing of their tools against stone are absent, the Passover throng produces a Tower of Babel-like cacophony of languages. At Passover, the number of people within Jerusalem swells to what must be one million--all speaking at once, I believe!

Languages swirl around me. The temple services are performed in Hebrew. Greek is the language of traders, aristocrats, and scholars. I also speak Aramaic, as do the people in the streets, and I know Latin enough to make a sale. And there are yet more dialects being spoken that I do not know.

Added to the sounds of the crowd are the loud cries of the other sellers announcing the ceremonial fitness of their animals--whose bleating and lowing and cooing also add to the din.

I ask my trusted friend, Akim, to watch my doves while I pay my tribute. His sheep are penned close enough that we may talk when times are slow--but times are not slow during the Passover.

Leaving the shade of the arched colonnades around the high outer walls, I enter the large outer court.

Herod has built up the temple mound, itself, to create a larger court than Solomon's. The Court of the Gentiles--called thus because Gentiles may enter the outer court and even offer sacrifices--is a huge square, with each outer edge at least nine hundred feet long. The Meeting Hall of the Sanhedrin makes up one side of the square. The other three are lined with the arched colonnades of the porticos providing shade; one of these, Solomon's Porch where my birds are shaded, is the only portion of Solomon's Temple not totally destroyed by Nebuchadnezzer.

In this large court, I must trade my ordinary coins, which are unacceptable as a temple offering because of the blasphemous markings upon them of the Roman emperor, who also claims deity. In exchange, the moneychanger gives me a silver Tyrian half-shekel, the shekel of the sanctuary, keeping the extra as his interest.

In the center of this outer court a large rectangle is formed by a low stone wall, the balustrade. At each opening, printed in red ink on the stones, in both Latin and Greek, is the warning: "*No foreigner may enter within the balustrade and enclosure around the Temple area. Anyone caught doing so will bear the responsibility for his own ensuing death.*"

I am glad the rulers allow no defilement of the temple from Gentiles entering close to the holy inner courts. The Romans allow us even to put to death a Roman citizen for so doing, though I am glad to say I have never witnessed such a spectacle.

Inside the boundary of the low stone wall balustrade is another rectangle formed by the tall walls of the inner courts. I pass through an opening in the balustrade, and climb the low flight of steps. Here the air is heavy with the odors of the sacrifices--the scent of blood, incense, and charred animal fat.

I enter through the center of three gates leading into the Court of the Women, called such because the women of Israel may enter here--but go no further. Only males may proceed through the magnificent Nicanor Gate into the Court of the Israelites, just as none but priests may proceed further into the Court of the Priests. And even the priests may not enter into the Holy of Holies in the heart of the complex, except one priest only, on the Day of Atonement.

But today I need not pass farther than the Court of the Women. Here I pay my acceptable coin to a priest, and watch as my name is written on the parchment and my Tyrian half-shekel deposited into one of the thirteen ram's-horn-shaped chests, later to be transferred to the Shekel Chamber.

There. My duty is done for the year. My tribute has been paid. I feel a sense of satisfaction as I retrace my steps, leaving the Court of Women and going down the stairs. Again I pass through the sacred boundary of the balustrade, and make my way through the clusters of people milling about in the large Court of the Gentiles. I continue to the edge of the court, back to the colonnades protecting my doves from the heat of the sun. I nod to Akim, and I watch his sheep as he goes to pay his own yearly tribute.

In the outer court and under the porticos of the outer walls, there are many others who, like me, make their living helping people make their sacrifices. Stalls are filled with bulls and oxen, pens with sheep, goats, and lambs, cages with turtledoves and pigeons.

None of the sacrifices made in this temple--for the redemption of the soul of a newborn child and atonement for the child's mother, the burnt offering, the peace offering, the sin offering, the trespass offering-- *none* could be performed without the animals which we sell.

Some do bring their own animals, but most depend upon us for this service. We sell them pure animals, without blemish, without injury or disfigurement, without disease--as decreed in God's Law. I do it for the pleasure of serving in the temple, but I admit there is also good money in helping others who travel from afar and cannot carry sacrificial animals with them.

And turtledoves are always in demand, for two are required for purification from uncleanness, and they are for the poor instead of a lamb.

Those too poor even for doves or pigeons give, in their place, the tenth part of an ephah of fine flour, and that also may be purchased here.

As Akim returns to his sheep, I watch a man enter through the gate into the Court of the Gentiles. He is followed by a small retinue. Though the grounds are thronged with people, yet my eyes are drawn to him. I have not seen him before, but my eyes keep coming back to him. That is a strange thing for me, for usually I watch alertly for buyers, and this man has not the look of a buyer.

When Akim sees where my gaze falls, he says, "The man is the carpenter's son, Jesus, descendant of the House of David. I have seen him here before and he does not buy of the animals. Pay him no mind."

Pay him no mind, Indeed. I look at the man anew. Of the revered royal House of David, from which the scriptures say the Messiah will descend. The man wears a sash of shepherd's plaid, for the head of the House of David is also King of the Shepherds. This man does have a look of nobility about him. Strong of body. Tall of stature. Brilliant of eye. And something more. His is indeed a commanding presence.

As I watch him scan the crowds in the temple grounds, I am struck by the sadness on his face. He shakes his head, as if in disbelief. But why? The temple grounds are the temple grounds and there is nothing new here. He is a Jew and of the House of David, not a foreigner, thus this cannot be his first time here. Yet he seems at odds with the calls of the moneychangers.

A man and woman stand before me, and I force my gaze to them. Before we consummate the deal on the two doves the couple needs, we haggle with gusto. I announce they will starve my three children and put me from my home with their offer. They say I bankrupt them with my price. I tell them a sacrifice of two such pure birds will fly straight to the heavens on unblemished wings. Finally, we agree on a price with which we are both pleased. I feel I have won and they do, as well. Such is the art of haggling.

As I pocket their coins and they carry away their pure, unblemished doves, I smile with my good fortune. I have already sold six birds this day, eight more still available for purchase, and many more in their cages at home. My wife will smile upon me this evening.

I cast my gaze about and see the man of David. It looks as though he weaves together small cords. But for what purpose? There is no use for cords in the temple, except perhaps to lead the oxen. Will he sacrifice an ox?

Why do I care? Again I drag my gaze from him and deliberately look elsewhere.

The cries of the other temple sellers fill my ears.

"Two pigeons for a senin..."

"Sacrifice the purest sheep in all the kingdom..."

"Good rates for your temple coins..."

I find my gaze drawn again. The man still plaits. I force my attention back to my business. I have more doves to sell before this day is through, and I intend to do so. Thus I add my voice to that of the others. *"Unblemished doves for sale. Your offering will fly on pure wings straight to heaven."*

I hear a commotion of voices raised in indignation. Surprised, I see the cause of it is the man of the House of David. He raises his arm and whips it down, sending coins scattering off a moneychanger's table and clattering onto the stones lining the courtyard.

What the man was plaiting earlier is a whip, a fearsome thing. But no more so than the man, himself, for he now seems to glow with a fearsome light that shines upward from where he stands. The sight sends shivers up my spine and tingles along my limbs. A man of light? How can that be?

Even his followers stand apart from him now, watching, appearing to wonder, as do I, what he does.

This Jesus does not stop with the coins. He also drives the oxen from their stalls, the sheep from their pens. He does not use the cord on the beasts, but they run as if they know he wants them out of the temple grounds. Women scream as the animals run past. Everywhere there is commotion.

Jesus overthrows a moneychanger's table and pours out the man's coins, as the moneychanger backs away. I know this moneychanger well, and if any other had overturned his table, he would have fought. But now he merely backs away in fear, and leaves the temple grounds, crying out for the rulers of the temple, the Sadducees. I am astounded, both at the unexpected action of the man of light and the surprising reaction of the moneychanger.

For a brief moment, there is silence, an amazing thing in this court filled with so many people and beasts in commotion. Then the whip cracks again, and more coins clink and fall onto the stones. Worried sheep bleat, as do those whose wares are overturned.

As the man of light makes his way through the tables of the moneychangers toward my cages, I hope he will not harm my delicate creatures. I want to stay to protect them, but I cannot. Almost without realizing, I find myself standing and backing away. Away from this man whose fierce wrath cannot be withstood. It is almost as if power from this man goes as a wall before him, pushing me back.

He pauses before my cages, but does not overturn them. When he stops, I am surprised to realize he is not out of control, as I first supposed. But his eyes burn with indignation as he looks at us who sell turtledoves and pigeons.

He motions toward the gate. *"Take these things hence."*

Relief floods me as I realize he will not harm my birds. Neither, I realize, has he harmed any of the other creatures. Nor the sellers.

Then to all, he says, loudly, with righteous anger carrying his voice above the din. *"Make not my Father's house a house of merchandise."*

His father's house? His ancestor, Solomon, son of David? Or...?

I have no time to ponder, as I hurriedly gather up my birds in their cages and wheel them on my cart from the temple, down the stairs, out into the street, and into the shade of the outside wall.

The man's words ring in my ears and pierce my heart. Have I defiled the temple by transacting my business therein? I have done nothing that others have not also done. But the guilt I feel does not depart with that thought.

The temple is the House of the Lord. Thus I have been one who has turned the House of the Lord into a house of merchandise, all the while saying I served therein. The lie sickens me as I see it for what it is.

Others just as guilty as I run out--carrying cages, leading oxen, herding sheep--their eyes surely as large as mine must also be.

The moneychangers are the ones most harshly dealt with, as their wares--their coins--are poured out by this man wielding the cords. Roman coins and Tyrian half-shekels alike, tossed to the ground, all unacceptable to him.

None stay to stop him. None dare to try. None seem able to breach his wall of power.

The man's disciples have been quiet, but one of them now cries out, "The zeal of thine house hath eaten me up." Another says, "Yes, I remember."

I also recognize the quote of the Psalmist. Its meaning has been debated much by the Rabbis. *Bitter enemies of thy temple tear me in pieces...Zeal for thy house will destroy me...The zeal of thine house hath consumed me.*

David wrote it while in exile, his the lone voice of righteousness in a wicked kingdom ruled by the wicked Saul, who had vowed to kill him. I know it is one of the Messianic psalms.

Is this man of light also a lone voice of righteousness in declaring this temple unclean? Do we live in a wicked kingdom ruled by wicked Sadducees and Pharisees?

Is he the Messiah?

I find I am pulled to this man of light in fascination. I ought to hide from his wrath. To leave this place. To watch over my doves. To take my earnings home and give them to my wife.

But I cannot. Just as I had to back away when he approached, now I find I am drawn to him. I leave behind my doves, something I never do, making sure they are in the shade. I *must* see this man again. I must listen to him.

He stands in the courtyard, tables strewn all around him, coins--which the owners dare not reclaim--lying in the dust at his feet.

There are others still in the courtyard, many others, but they are speechless, as am I.

For the time of a blink of an eye, there is total silence except for the man's heavy breathing as he catches his breath. Finally, with the temple's outer courts cleared of animals and sellers, he tosses his whip aside.

When he looks toward where I stand, I shrink back, fearing his wrath. Yet he does not look angry. Instead, there is that same sadness in his gaze. And, when his eyes find mine, I see...*love*?

I am shaken to my core.

If this man of light is of the House of David, and claims this is his father's house, then is he the Messiah proclaimed in the scriptures to come forth in these days?

I cannot pull my eyes from his, and my limbs begin to tremble with the joy I feel.

Indeed, I know in this moment that the Messiah has come.

Into His Father's house.

About His Father's business.

To save His Father's children.

As prophesied by Abraham and Isaiah and Moses and all the prophets from the time of Adam.

The guilt I felt earlier at having defiled the Lord's temple fades, replaced by the love from this man's gaze. I drop to my knees to worship the Messiah.

Angry Sadducees hurry from the Meeting Hall, searching out the cause of the commotion. Pharisees move closer from their place in the courtyard. Jesus moves His gaze from me, and I feel the loss. As He turns toward them, they stop, obviously afraid to go hence.

"What sign showest thou unto us, seeing that thou doest these things?" The haughty voice of the Sadducee is filled with the anger and hatred that I did not hear in the voice of the Messiah even while He cleared the temple. Cleansed it. And even the priest knows the temple needed cleansing, for he does not ask why Jesus has done so, but only by what authority.

The Messiah answers them, "Destroy this temple, and in three days I will raise it up."

Then says another Sadducee scornfully, "Forty and six years was this temple in building, and wilt thou rear it up in three days?"

But I do not think Jesus speaks of this temple of Solomon, of Herod, but of the temple of His body. The Sadducees do not believe in resurrection and immortality as do the Pharisees, but the Pharisees together with the Sadducees pretend to misunderstand.

Do they not remember Jonah, who the mariners cast into the sea, and the Lord had prepared a great fish to swallow? Do they not remember Jonah was in the belly of the great fish three days and three nights? Do they not recall the Lord then spake to the fish, and it vomited Jonah upon the dry land? The Messiah refers to the sign of Jonah in regard to himself. Will He then rise after three days? But why does He speak of His death? None can breach His wall of power, not even the rulers who stand so incensed before Him.

One of the Sadducees murmurs, "Blasphemer!"

I stay rooted to the spot. Though the Sadducees and Pharisees are angry, they stand aside when Jesus climbs upon the steps of Solomon's porch and begins to preach to His disciples. The crowd around him grows, as others, like myself, are drawn to Him.

As I listen to His words, an urgency fills me. I must share this news with my wife and children!

I return to my doves, thankful to find Akim watching over them, his small flock of sheep herded into the corner of a neighboring building. He is also amazed.

When I pull my cart home, my wife asks why I am home early. My children gather round to watch me put my doves away, and I say with joy, "I have much to share with you this day, Woman. The Messiah has come."

At her gasp, I smile. So He has. My heart swells with joy as I remember His care not to harm my doves or the other animals, His love for me, the power that went before Him, pushing us back where we should have been to start.

The Lord will guide me to find another place to set up my cages that will not be offensive to the Father or His Son. Outside the walls of the temple. Perhaps my business will do better there, as I will be the first dove-seller the crowds encounter. But regardless, it shall be done, even if I have to build a canopy to shade my doves.

I will not be found in the wrong place again.

I smile at my wife, who still does not understand, and reach for her hand and then motion for my children. I will take them with me, to listen to the Man of David, the Man of Light, the very Messiah, for themselves. Then they will know what I cannot put into words, but Isaiah did.

The Sun of righteousness has arisen with healing in His wings.

Indeed.

And when they could not come
nigh unto Him for the press, they
uncovered the roof where He was:
and when they had broken it up,
they let down the bed
wherein the
sick of the palsy lay.

(Mark 2:4)

TAKE UP THY BED
Man Sick of the Palsy

My mother wipes the drool from my cheeks, pats my head gently, and says, "Zuriel, I will return soon."

Zuriel. *Stone.* When my mother named me for one of the polished stones she loves to collect and which still line her windows, she could not see into the future when I would lie here unmoving as a rock.

I live in Capernaum. Or, rather, my family lives in Capernaum. I simply exist. I lived here once, when my body went where I instructed it to go. But now it does not follow any commands but those of chaos.

Now I merely exist and my existence is my bed. Others around me must care for me. They must ladle life-sustaining nourishment down my throat. They must clean up after me. They must even help me cough.

That is not life.

But it helps me to know that others love me enough to care for me.

41

My family does care for me and does love me, though I can tell I am a burden. I can no longer even speak my thanks to them. I am as useless as my body.

Once I was as other men, walking about on two legs. But now I am moved upon. In the hot weather, others must heft me to the roof when we sleep there to catch the breeze. Others must carry me to the garden behind my house or the street before it. I am tied to the four walls of this house.

As my painful, twisted body lies here, my mind races. It often does.

Others wonder what sin I have committed that my body has become so useless. Useless as a newborn babe's, but much more painful. Heaven knows when I was able, I did sin. And I have ample time now to think back over my sins and regret them. But is it the commission of the sins I regret, or the fact they have brought upon me the ruin of my body?

I wonder why I cannot die. What point is there in my being in this state?

A man calls out an excited greeting. It is my friend Abraham, named after the great prophet and father of our nation. "Zuriel, this is your lucky day."

I turn my eyes, for they alone still do my bidding.

Abraham laughs as my father, my uncle, and my brother follow him in. "Oh, yes, Zuriel. I know you do not think you are the lucky one, but today you are."

I had many friends once, friends I would not have my parents see with me. Now I need not fear--they were friends of the foolishness of my youth and care not for any save themselves and their vain pleasures. Their sins have not ruined their bodies, but perhaps their spirits.

My father's face is bright. "The Master, Jesus, is in Capernaum. Even now many are going to Him to be healed of their infirmities. And today we take you."

I look at these four men, these who have stood beside me even though I did not live as I should and have been thus punished. Oh, how I wish I had not brought shame and pain to each of them.

"Did you not hear us?" my uncle asks. "You do not look as excited as you ought."

Abraham laughs. "He never seems excited any more. But that will all change today, when the Master but utters a word and he is healed."

I know who the Master is, this Jesus of Nazareth of whom they speak, for my father and my mother are believers. They speak of Him oft.

The Master will know what I have done to bring this upon myself. He will look upon me and see this is the fitting state in which a sinner such as I belong.

I close my eyes. How can I tell them I do not wish to go before the Master? I do not wish to see in the eyes of this Jesus that He knows my sins.

"Wake up, my friend," whispers Abraham and I open my eyes to find his face close to mine. He smiles mischievously. "You will be healed today. Open your eyes and rejoice."

43

I would speak, if I could. I would smile, if I could. I would even rejoice, which I can do, except I am afraid for what the Master will say to a sinner.

But, for my friend's sake, and for my father's and mother's and uncle's and brother's, I will open my eyes and pretend to rejoice. For I know Abraham enough to know if he is determined to take me to the Master, no amount of mere eye rolling will keep me here.

They simply heft my bed, one at each corner. I know I must have wasted away until I am not much of a burden to carry, for they lift easily.

My sins, however, are a heavy burden that I, without strength, must carry alone.

As I am moved through the streets, we join others going the same way. And, soon, we come upon a crowd of people. A multitude.

The four carrying me stop. My father mutters, "We cannot go forward."

Abraham, never to be deterred, stays positive. "We will go around, then."

And so we go around, but we find the crowd as dense and unpassable here.

Relief begins to bud within me. The Master will not see me, after all. My sins will remain hidden, locked in my body, keeping me from moving, weighing down my heart as the sickness weighs down my limbs and twists them unnaturally.

I look up at Abraham. He grins and says, "My good friend Zuriel, do not despair. We will find a way to get you to the Master."

They begin to look around, to search for such a way.

It does not take them long to walk all around the house. The crowd fills every doorway, every window. There is no way through.

We stop and I see beads of sweat on the brows of my father and uncle. Abraham wipes his brow, as well. The pallet upon which I exist must be heavy, then.

"Who are these people?" my brother asks.

My uncle answers, "Everyone is here. I see Pharisees and doctors of the law sitting by, and I see people of our village and from other villages round about."

The crowd shuffles around and an old man comes from the house, a man blind for many years. When I could move, I tossed coins in his cup. Now he has a glorious smile upon his face and points at the trees, and at the people, and at objects in turn. *He can see!* The Master has healed him!

But healing eyes is not the same as healing a twisted and wasted body and making it new again.

Soon after, a woman comes forth, crying, "I am well again!"

I have no doubt Jesus is *The* Healer. I know He can heal me, as well, and I fight against the hope that this knowledge brings. The blind man and sick woman never lived a life of great sin as did I. The Master doubtless was glad to help them.

Tears sting my eyes, and I blink them back. I am glad for these people, but I also wish this healing for myself. Part of me wants to be carried in with the hope of walking out, but the other part of me wants to be taken home, to hide in my bed and try to forget the sins that weigh so heavily upon my soul.

When Abraham exclaims, "Ah, ha," I know he thinks he has found a solution to our problem. The crowd must be thinning and he has seen a way into the house. "Let us go up, brothers."

I am jostled. My father places his hand so the sun is not in my eyes.

We do not go toward the front of the house, but to the side. To the stairway. Abraham said up. I thought . . . but with Abraham it does not do well to think. He acts. Often impetuously.

Soon I have been jostled up onto the roof. The men set my pallet down, and I can feel the heat from the sun above on my face and from the roof underneath. I close my eyes again.

My uncle says, "The bed will not fit through the trapdoor."

Most roofs have trapdoors and, no, I am sure my pallet would not fit down through any of them. Surely they do not mean to lower me down?

But, surely, that is exactly what Abraham has in mind. "We will enlarge it."

And soon I hear tiles being removed.

When the sounds cease, I can hear the voice of the Master coming from within the house.

His voice is deep and low, yet carries easily. It floats upon the breeze. The voice of the man who can heal my body and see into my soul and sinful heart.

And I realize in that moment that I do deeply regret the sins, themselves, and not just that they have turned my body to ruin. *I would give anything to come before Jesus clean, to have a pure heart for Him to look into.*

Abraham comes to me and, for once, does not smile. "Zuriel, we will get you to the Master. He will heal you. Do you understand?"

I blink so he knows I understand his words.

"Good." He lays his large, rough hand upon my cheek. "And then you will be yourself once again."

No, not myself. Never again myself, for myself was too much a sinner. A new man, perhaps. A wiser, purer man. Never myself again.

My father and my uncle and my brother and my friend each tie a cord onto the corners of my bed, and the pallet swings into the air.

I cannot control my body, neither can I control my fear. What happens if my body falls? I will not feel the fall, but will the fall end my life?

And suddenly I want to live, to see the Master, even if He turns away. Despite my efforts to keep it in check, hope flickers as a small flame in my chest.

I sway down, down, down. Through the ragged opening in the roof, I see the faces of the men who love me peering down, their hands holding tight to the cords suspending me.

As I descend, more things come into view. Surprised faces. Furniture. A crowd of enormity in this room, alone.

The face of the Master. I am here, now, before Him. He and I are in the center of the crowd.

The Master is looking up at my family and friend, and can surely see their love for me and their faith in Him, can surely see what good men they are.

Then He moves His gaze to me, and I feel the muscles around my eyes tense. But as He looks into my eyes, deep enough to see my sins, to see what an unrighteous man I have been, I do not see the censure I expected. His lips do not curl with disdain nor call out my sins.

Instead I see such love that my breath catches and a warmth fills me as far as I can feel.

My pallet touches the floor.

"Son, be of good cheer." The Master smiles and speaks gently, reaching down to touch my twisted claw of a hand. "Thy sins be forgiven thee."

He knows I have sinned. He knows and loves me still. And He says I am forgiven of my sins. At His words, a dark weight lifts from my heart and floats up through the hole in the roof above me, gone forever.

I take a deep breath, my heart no longer pinned as tightly as before. He has forgiven me my sins and wants me to go my way and sin no more.

I cannot go my way, but I *can* sin no more. My heart rejoices. I expected a different sort of healing, but this is the healing I needed. A healing of my broken heart and contrite spirit. A healing from my sin-laden state.

I am not ready to leave His presence--I have never been so loved--but the others were sent out immediately after their healing. And my healing is done.

Others in the room murmur and for a moment I look upon their faces and can almost see their thoughts. Perhaps it is my nearness to the Master, the healing He has just wrought upon me, for I sense they wonder how Jesus can forgive my sins, for only God can do so.

I see Jesus has heard the men's thoughts and perceived their reasoning within themselves, for he says unto them, "Why reason ye these things in your hearts? Whether is it easier to say to the sick of the palsy, 'Thy sins be forgiven thee' or to say, 'Arise, and take up thy bed and walk'?"

He looks down at me and again I feel His love for me, and also for these other sinners who sit nearby, questioning in their hearts.

The Master looks around the crowd and all is silent for a moment. Finally, He says, quietly, so that all strain to hear, "But that ye may know that the Son of Man hath power on earth to forgive sins--"

He looks into my eyes again, and I see that He truly is the Son of Man, the Son of the Most High, the Messiah, and I know He has truly forgiven my sins, for I feel the light and lightness in my heart.

He continues, "I say unto thee, *Arise, and take up thy bed, and go thy way into thine house.*"

And immediately the pain in my limbs is gone. I look down--*I can move my head!*--to see my limbs which I must use to obey His command. My hands no longer resemble claws but look as other men's. My legs and feet are straight and strong.

I am healed! I can do as Jesus instructed!

Immediately I do arise. Savoring the lack of pain and jerky movements. Smoothly, as if there was never a period of time when I wasted and twisted, my body responds to my mind. I am healed, as were the others who earlier left the house rejoicing. I am healed, both body and soul, mind and spirit, inside and out.

And I can speak! Over and over, I say, "Thank you, Lord. Thank you."

As I recover from my initial astonishment, I take up my bed, as Jesus commanded, and go forth.

The people in the crowd are all amazed, and many glorify God and are filled with fear, saying, "We never saw it on this fashion."

"We never saw the power of God after this manner."

"We have never seen a healing such as this."

"We have seen strange things today."

I, the strange thing they have seen today, walk upright on strong limbs and straight joints.

And I, as those before, cannot help from calling out to the crowd, "I am healed! Jesus has made me whole!"

As I come out through the crowd, I search the faces for the men with the faith to bring me here this day.

My father. My uncle. My brother. My friend.

They come running down the stairs and surround me, rejoicing with me.

Abraham, like the big bear he resembles, takes me in a hug and swings me around and then sets my feet upon the ground.

My father's face crumples with his tears of joy as he takes me into his embrace for a long moment.

My uncle cannot stop saying, over and over, "It is a miracle! It is a miracle!"

My brother punches my arm as he has not done for many years. I punch his in return, and then stop, and look at them all, love overflowing its bounds.

I speak to them the words I have wanted to say for these many years. "I love you all. Thank you for everything you have done for me."

And now even Abraham is wiping his cheeks, and I am wiping mine.

"And now, I must obey the command of the Master, and go into my house."

Again I pick up my bed from which I have been freed and walk toward my home and my mother.

I will go and sin no more. I do not wish to ever bring upon myself infirmity again with my sins.

But, even more important, when I look into the eyes of the Messiah again, I wish Him to see that I have kept myself as pure, righteous, and free from sin as possible since He forgave me this day.

I am cleansed and healed of all my sins.

Hallelujah! Thank Heaven for a Savior who sees our sins and loves us still.

Come out of the man,
thou unclean spirit.

(Mark 5:8)

LEGION

Man From Whom Jesus Casts The Unclean Spirits

"We can break free," a voice calls out.

"Let me pull on the fetters," cries another, plucking at the chains binding us.

A third yells, "I can do it!"

They are many, The Others. They are loud and greedy and angry. Always so angry. They seem never to cease their talking, first one, then another, sometimes all at once.

I have become lost in the crowd. My voice is gone. Even my name is forgotten.

I wish they would stop their yelling. But noise is what they are desperate for. Noise is but one way they have of feeling alive, always more alive, more painfully alive. They grasp at noise and pain.

Some crave the feeling of the stones under our bare feet, and the bruises that result.

Others ache for the feel of the cold and wind and rain on our bare skin, and therefore we have worn no clothing for a long time. Many want to eat, always eat, until I am sick. They even like to experience that.

And they all together do not want to sleep, for then the sensations end, and so I am always exhausted. Even when I do finally sleep, the nightmare continues.

The outside ones have tried to stop The Others, but they cannot. I cannot stop them, either. They have grown too strong. They are too many.

The outside ones speak of our fierceness and how The Others frighten them from passing this way. So the outside ones have put us again into chains, but even now the fingers of The Others, their strength combined, pluck the chains asunder and break the fetters in pieces. No man can tame us, though many have tried. But always we escape.

And so we stand, free of the chains, again. But I am not free of my chains.

One of The Others howls in triumph.

My throat burns.

We run across the rocky ground, back to the safety of the tombs.

My feet ache.

We sit on the cool ground outside our cave.

My skin is cold and I shiver.

But still The Others are not satisfied. There must always be more, more, *forever more*.

54

More sensation. More feeling. More pain.

One of The Others picks up a stone. This one likes to feel alive by getting our heart pumping and by bleeding, and he rips the stone along our arm until we bleed. He yips in aliveness.

My arm stings.

We are in the country of the Gadarenes and Gergesenes, but we no longer live in my house or any house. We dwell amongst the tombs, the caves where the dead are kept.

And I am as dead and as if in hell, yet am I not dead at all but constantly reminded by The Others that we are alive and bleeding, alive and screaming, alive and cold, alive and bruised. Alive. Painfully alive.

One of The Others shrieks with anger because the bleeding has stopped.

My throat throbs.

I see a man afar off, and The Others recognize him. We run and The Others fling down our body and worship the man. I feel their longing, and also their fear cold around me.

Who is this man The Others fear?

One of The Others cries out with a loud voice, "What have I to do with thee, Jesus, thou Son of the Most High God? I beseech thee, torment me not."

This man before us is the Son of the Most High God? How do The Others know what I do not?

This Jesus asks me, "What is thy name?"

He speaks softly, yet The Others recognize the command in his voice, as do I, and we rush to declare our name. But I no longer remember my name. The noise is too confusing, The Others too greedy to let me remember, to keep my own self.

One of The Others speaks. "My name is Legion; for we are many."

And The Others beseech Jesus much that He send them not away out of the country.

They mean me. I am that country in which they live and feel alive.

If I could only find my voice, I would ask that He send these devils away. Can this Son of the Most High God save me? *Help! Please help me!*

The Others are frantic now. They search around and see, nigh unto the mountains, a great herd of swine feeding. I have overheard the swine herders say there are two thousand of the unclean animals there.

The Others together beg this Jesus, saying, "If thou cast us out, suffer us to go away into the herd of swine."

Jesus looks into my eyes and I am shaken. A great peace--one I never felt before, even before The Others--comes over me. Love surrounds me as if I am wrapped in a blanket of it.

Why are The Others so agitated when Jesus brings such peace? Such joy? Such love?

And forthwith Jesus gives them leave to enter the swine--*poor swine!*--and then He says to those who are with me, "Come out of the man, thou unclean spirit."

When Jesus thus commands, I feel a rushing as the many others leave this country that is my body, and I feel the rift healed around me that allowed them to enter me years ago.

The silence inside me is amazing!

There is no contention within.

No anger. No arguing. No yelling.

In my head is only quiet. In my heart is only incredible peace. In my body is only I. And only I determine where my body will go, what it will do.

As I continue to gaze into the eyes of Jesus, I feel the warmth of His great compassion for me. Perhaps I am sensitive to goodness because I have been so long surrounded by evil, but I perceive this man to be of purity and light. Of love.

And in that instant also I feel my body healed. My throat no longer aches. My arm that was bleeding has no scratch left upon it. The bruises have left my feet.

And I am naked!

Jesus smiles at me and I am filled with light. He places His hand upon my shoulder. Instead of aching and cold, I feel peace and a loving warmth.

Jesus wraps a robe around my shoulders to hide my nakedness.

One of His disciples raises his arm. "*Look!*"

And I do look--I, myself, alone at last--and see the two thousand swine. They are now agitated and I can see The Others have entered them. And the swine run violently down a steep place into the sea, and perish in the waters.

I am relieved they are gone from me. That even the swine do not have to endure what I did, for death is better than the devils.

It has happened so quickly it is amazing. The swine are gone, but I am still here. The Others have now felt of a body's death as well as its aliveness. And I am relieved it is not my death they feel. Nor my aliveness, ever again.

The pigs could not endure, but I have survived. I have been saved from my awful state. My heart swells with love for the Son of the Most High God who has saved me. My Savior.

Before The Others, I had heard of the Messiah, but I never expected Him to come searching for me in the midst of my confusion, to take me by the hand and lead me home. To safety. To love. To myself.

They that feed the swine flee, and go their ways into the city to tell everything that has taken place. They stare at me, and point, and I believe they will also tell what has befallen the man who was before possessed of the devils.

And the disciples of The Savior take me into the sea and wash my body, for it has not been bathed for these many years the devils were within me, and I stink.

Surprised, I feel no fear of The Others, who ran with the swine into the water in which I now bathe. The rift is healed and I am safe. They can never again enter and I will never again harbor any thoughts that could invite them or re-open the rift.

After I am cleansed, the apostles lead me from the waters and dry me, and give unto me clean clothes.

These men are not like The Others. They are loud, yes, but without anger, without greed, without grasping. They are large and noisy, but also gentle and kind.

Being in their presence brings me continued peace.

We sit in a circle and talk. They feed me and I find I am hungry for good food.

Gratitude fills me that the Son of the Most High God would heal me from my affliction. That He would then speak with me, as one man speaks with another. And I can answer Him, with my own voice. With my own heart. With my own mind clear enough as I look into His eyes that my name returns to my mind.

I am no longer Legion!

I am Arion, son of Aaron and Jerusha, who are gone already to Paradise. The memory brings me joy and yet a pang of sadness that my parents are gone. Though I am thus alone, I wonder at being filled with light after so many years of darkness.

It is truly a miracle.

Now I am in the light, I will guard my mind against thoughts of darkness. I will seek after light each day.

We speak for a long time, and then the people of the city--it must be the whole city, there are so many--come out to meet Jesus.

And when they who before chained me now see me, who was possessed with Legion, sitting and clothed and in my right mind, I see the fear in their eyes.

And I hear those who saw the miracle retell how it befell me, who was possessed with the devils and how the devils were cast out, and also concerning the swine.

And then the whole multitude of the country of the Gadarenes round about begins to beseech Jesus to depart from them, for they are taken with great fear.

But they know not the meaning of true fear for they have never dwelt among The Others.

How can they want Jesus gone? My heart is drawn to His light, His love, His peace.

His very deed of saving me speaks of His righteousness, and I sense these people from the city are unrighteous and thus they fear miracles. They want no miracles here.

But I *am* one of His miracles!

As Jesus walks to the shore, to respect the wishes of the crowd, and goes up into a ship, I ask Him if I might go with Him. That I, too, might be a disciple who wanders with Him. That I may see more of His miracles. That I may show myself as His miracle and help people believe His words.

Jesus looks pleased with my desire to share my story with others. He says, "Go home to thy *friends*, and tell *them* how great things the Lord hath done for thee, and hath had compassion on thee." He looks deeply into my eyes and smiles and I am filled again with His loving light. "Yes. Return to thine own house, and show how great things God hath done unto thee."

"As you say so will I do, Lord." I step back from the shore. I watch as Jesus enters the ship, and as the sails are raised, and as He passes over unto the other side, unto Capernaum.

Only then do I depart.

I will go as my Savior has spoken. I will travel throughout the whole region, the district of Perea, into the cities of Gadara, and Gerasa, and Gergesa, throughout Decapolis. I will do as Jesus has commanded me, and I will tell all who will listen--and some who will not!--the great things Jesus has done for me.

That the very Son of the Most High God took me from the darkness of my affliction and brought me into His light and healed me, body and soul.

And all those who hear me will marvel at the tale.

But none more than I, Arion, son of Aaron and Jerusha.

And He said, 'Go forth, and stand upon the mountain before the Lord.'
And, behold, the Lord *passed by*, and a great and strong wind rent the mountains, and brake in pieces the rocks before the Lord; but the Lord was not in the wind.
And after the wind an earthquake; but the Lord was not in the earthquake.
And after the earthquake a fire; but the Lord was not in the fire.
And after the fire a still small voice.

(1ˢᵗ Kings 19:11-12)

And He saw them toiling in rowing; for the wind was contrary unto them; and about the fourth watch of the night He cometh unto them, walking upon the sea, and would have *passed by* them.

(Mark 6:48)

A LITTLE FAITH
Peter Walks with Christ

The wind shrieks about me and I cling to the rope tied around me to keep from being swept overboard. It has been thus most of the night.

I am Peter and I take another turn rowing, for the wind goes against us. I grasp the wooden oar in both hands and pull with all my strength.

Andrew, whose turn it is to rest, falls back exhausted against the side of the boat and strains to fill his lungs with something besides water. He tangles his arm in the ropes, as well, to anchor himself.

We row in rhythm, fighting with our feet and legs to stay upright when the big waves hit our ship, one after another, every few seconds, wave after wave.

Even as we fight to stay afloat, the shriek of the wind and the howl of the waves grows louder.

Why did Jesus constrain us to get into the ship and go to the other side, unto Bethsaida and Capernaum? After He sent away the people who would have taken

Him by force to make Him a King, even that same five thousand He fed with the five loaves and the two fishes, He went into the mountain without us. Who now will bring Him across to us?

I know not.

The more pressing question is if we will make it through this night with our ship and our lives intact.

I have seen storms before. The other apostles--many of whom are seasoned fishermen, like unto myself--have battled their share of storms, and brought ships in safely despite the waves and wind.

But only one other time have any of us seen waves like these, clawing at the ship as though to drag us under into a watery grave. Wind that howls like a wild beast hungry for our flesh. But this night we are alone. Our Lord is not here, even if we had need to wake Him from sleep as before, to command the waves and the winds to be still.

The wind chills my skin, but I shiver from the fear that has settled deep within my chest, from the wetness of the waves and my work of rowing as I pull the oars in rhythm with the others. Pull. Lift. Pull. Lift.

Pull.

Lift.

We are relatively young men, in our prime, but this storm is punishing us and pushing us to our limits.

I do not think we can survive much longer without sinking.

If only our Lord were here with us. He could calm the storm, as He did once before.

We have rowed five and twenty furlongs, maybe thirty, fighting the wind and the waves with every pull of the oars, yet we seem no closer to shore. At this rate, we will sink before we reach solid land.

The sky is dark except for bursts of lightning that illuminate the way. Our lantern that hangs over the water has been blown out. Clouds bunch and move and shift, as though they are waves above.

This is the fourth watch of the night, when the night sky begins to lighten with the dawn, yet I fear we will not survive to see the sun rise today.

My turn to row over, I stumble to the place where Andrew had lain, gasping for breath and taking my turn at clinging to the ropes to keep from being swept overboard. Water sloshes around me on the deck. Water slaps my face and tries to snatch my breath. Water clings to me and tries to pull me from the ship.

Finally, having caught my breath, I struggle to my feet to see if there is any break in the clouds, yet there is none. Only waves higher than our ship. I have seen many storms in my years as fisherman, but the sight before me chills my heart.

When lightning flashes again, I see a figure walking on the water.

"It is a spirit," we cry out together, of one mind in our fear, our combined voices barely heard.

My soul is sore troubled as the sky begins to lighten--strangely, for there is still no sun. But I can now see the figure clearly, striding upon the water as though a man walking upon earth, the waves heaving to and fro around Him, but stable beneath His feet.

Straightway upon our seeing the spirit, it speaks.

"Be of good cheer," the welcome voice of our Master comes, relieving my fear somewhat. "It is I. Be not afraid."

Our Master? Walking upon the waters? I have seen the incredible power of His priesthood before and I have watched Him command the elements.

I wait for Him to calm the waves and the wind, but He does not speak again, only stands firm and still on the surface water as it roils about Him.

A strange mixture of fear and excitement fills me. My heart burns within me, a desire to join my Lord, no matter how high the waves. I know it is my Lord and I also know I cannot walk on water without His command--but if Jesus commands me to walk on the waves, then He also commands the waves to firm beneath my feet and hold my weight. "Lord, if it be thou, bid me come unto thee on the water."

Through the darkness and torrents of rain, I see Jesus' face clearly, and He smiles upon me. "Come."

His look takes away my fear.

The other apostles are silent behind me, but perhaps they cannot yell loudly enough to be heard above the wind. Clinging to the ropes, I pay them no mind, my focus now only on Jesus. I am astounded. He walks upon the waters. He commands the elements and they obey. He commands me and I obey.

I hold tight to the boat as it continues to pitch and roll, as I throw my legs over the side, and climb down the outside of the boat, all without taking my eyes from Jesus. When my feet touch the surface of the waves, His smile urges me on, as if He is pleased with me.

My heart is full of fear, but I look into the eyes of my Savior and feel His love for me and His pleasure with my decision. A great calm comes over me as I look upon His face and know He has commanded the waves to hold me.

And they do! I take a step and the water holds firm beneath my feet. Another step. A third.

I walk upon the water! I am walking toward my Lord and Master. My heart rejoices in that which I could not do without Jesus.

He stands still while I walk toward Him, as though watching a tottering babe, which I am. A tottering babe upon the waves. A tottering babe in the ways of faith required to walk on water.

Yet a tottering babe daring to take a step. Joy fills my heart.

A wave slaps against me and I hear the roar of the wind that drives the waves before it. I still walk upon the water, but now I raise my hands as if to shield myself. I watch for the next wave . . . and I begin to sink.

My fear returns. My feet are covered with water. My ankles. My knees. The water is pulling me down, as it has fought to do for hours. Though I am a strong swimmer, I could not swim back to the boat. I will drown, no matter how far I could swim in calm water. I cry out for help. "Lord, save me."

Immediately Jesus stretches forth His hand, and catches my arm and pulls me up, my feet once again resting on the surface. He shakes His head and says, "O thou of little faith, wherefore didst thou doubt?"

But I feel no reproach in His words. He merely states the truth: I had only a little faith and so I began to sink. Still I feel His pleasure that I had enough faith- -smaller than a mustard seed though it may be--to get out of the boat, to walk thus far. My fear leaves me as I stare into the eyes of Jesus, who smiles at me again.

I am filled with His love for me, even though I am of little faith.

And then, together, we walk back to the ship, the Master and His apostle, upon the waves. With Him beside me, I can do anything. With Christ, truly all things are possible.

In the instant we come into the ship, the boisterous wind ceases. Without the wind, the waves disappear. The dark clouds lighten and part and the rays of the sun ready to be born tint the sky with faint color.

And I am amazed. Obviously, Jesus commanded the wind to cease, as He commanded the waves to hold me. But He did not command it to cease until after I walked with Him on the waves.

Why? Why did He have me walk in faith during the storm when He could have calmed the storm at any moment? So I would learn that He will buoy me up and keep me safe? I will ponder this in my heart.

As amazing as are my steps upon the water, immediately the ship is at the land whither we were going.

The apostles are amazed beyond measure and wonder, as do I, that our Lord walked upon the waves. I am amazed, as are they, that one of us also walked upon the waves, if only for a moment. They are amazed, as am I, that our ship could immediately reach shore.

The others join me in worshiping our Lord. "Of a truth, thou art the Son of God."

I look at my Lord again, and He smiles at me, pleased with my faulty performance.

As am I. I may be of little faith, still I am the only one with faith enough to climb from the boat and take a step.

I feared, yet still I stepped forth upon the waves.

It seemed not possible, yet I stepped forth upon the waves.

I asked to hear my Master's command, and I stepped forth upon the waves.

I will remember this night forever, and my soul will rejoice in the remembering.

I walked upon the heaving water with my Lord and He kept me safe upon it!

Bring thy son hither.

(Luke 9:41)

A FATHER'S PLEA
Man Whose Faith Wavers

Hope burns within my heart as my only son sits on the ground at the feet of the apostles.

Nathan, my gift from God.

I have brought him to the Master Healer, Jesus of Nazareth, but He is not here. The apostles say He went upon the mountain during the night, and also took with Him Peter, James, and John.

In answer to my plea that their MJune 27, 2005aster help my son, the remaining Apostles assure me the Healer has given them authority to cast out demons, and that they have indeed cast out many.

My relief at their words is great, for my son has for a long time had a demon that makes him dumb, unable

71

to speak. The demon has also tried to destroy my child many times.

This has been a great trial in my life and in my marriage. My wife has never stopped mourning the loss of this, our only child. Though he lives in our home still, he is as lost to us. When my wife looks upon him, I see the pain in her eyes and feel her withdraw from the world. She can no longer bear the pain nor the shame, for she feels it is our sins which have caused our child thus to suffer and has kept any other from coming to our home.

She would not come with us today for she is afraid even to hope.

And so I have brought my son here, to be healed by the man known as the Physician. His apostles are now my last hope.

I stand behind my seated son. The apostles stand before him. And a large crowd surrounds us all, my son in the center like the hub of a giant wheel.

One of the apostles steps to the center of the group. I hold my breath, waiting for the forthcoming miracle. The man confidently commands the demon to depart from my boy.

I wait, my heart full of hope, for a long moment.

My son looks in my direction, and I see the instant in which the demon attacks him yet again. Nathan falls to the ground and froths at the mouth, and my heart drops.

The apostles look perplexed. Many in the crowd seem to be upset at the sight of the attack upon my son. I am not surprised, as even to those accustomed to the sight, my son's fits are disturbing.

The group around us contains many lawyers and scribes this morning, and they love to contend with the apostles. They love to contend with *all*, and doubtless that is why they are become lawyers and scribes.

"You have no power over demons," one mocks. "Your failure only proves your lies."

"We have cast out demons before," Thomas insists, and Andrew echoes his words with, "We *can* cast them out."

Another apostle steps forward, and again the demon is commanded--through the power of the Most High God--to depart. But once again this only brings more agitation into my son. If they do not stop commanding soon, they might bring on the death this demon has so many times already tried to deliver to my son.

I kneel and wait for the attack to pass.

Finally, Nathan lies still upon the ground, his breathing shallow and rapid. Gently I push back his dark curls from his face as I draw in a deep breath and I do battle with the tears that would flow freely. I had hoped the apostles would have the power to do as they said they could. I believed!

Yet now I fear I must return to a life where my boy is here and yet not. A world where the last vestige of hope has been torn from my breast. A world where I must return to my child's mother and watch her sink further and further into her own awful mourning.

The voices swirl above me, as I sit on the ground by my son, steeped in my own despair. The apostles continue to debate among themselves why they are unable to do what they have done in the past.

I wonder if my sin that caused my son to have a demon is so great that even the apostles could not overcome it. Is it a sin I remember? Or have I done more wrong than I know?

Or, as my cousin claims, do sins not cause such problems? I have no answer. I know only my deep disappointment and anguish.

The scribes continue to question and contend. I listen not to the words. Obviously words cannot help my boy, even words spoken in command.

I help my son to sit. He does not yet recognize me. When he has these fits it takes time for him to come back to his senses. He is never fully here, but some times are definitely better than others.

I draw in another deep breath and climb to my feet. It is time to carry my son home, though I would rather walk on hot coals than to do so. There is nothing I would not do rather than face my wife and her new grief at this failure of the apostles.

Suddenly there is a commotion and the crowd begins to run away from us, toward the mount. I stand and catch a glimpse, between those running, of the Master and His three Apostles walking down the hill.

The other apostles and the lawyers are still contending with one another, even as they salute Him.

Jesus, whose face seems almost to glow, looks at the crowd, at the apostles and at the scribes, and asks, "What question ye with them?"

Since the argument has been about the healing or nonhealing of my son, I stand. Hope rises within me again at the sight of the Master. Perhaps He can do what His apostles could not.

I run to reach Him, and kneel at His feet. "Master, I have brought unto thee my son, which hath a dumb spirit." I point to my son. "Master, I beseech thee, look upon my son, for he is mine only child."

As I point, the crowd parts so that Jesus may see my son, who still sits dazed upon the ground behind us all.

"Lord, have mercy on my son," I plead, "for he is lunatic, and sore vexed. Lo, a spirit taketh him, and he suddenly crieth out; and it teareth him that he foameth again, and bruising him hardly departeth from him. Ofttimes he falleth into the fire, and oft into the water."

Nathan falls over into the dirt and lies there quietly, unaware. Waiting for the next attack.

"And I besought thy disciples to cast the spirit out." My heart rends within me and I struggle to keep the anguish from my voice and the tears from my eyes. "And they could not."

Jesus shakes His head sadly as He turns His gaze to His Apostles. "O faithless and perverse generation, how long shall I be with you? How long shall I suffer you?" He motions toward Nathan and says, "Bring thy son hither."

My hope flickers higher. Not so strongly as at first with the apostles, but yet it is there.

I hurry to my dazed son, help him to his feet, and lead him toward the Master.

But as we are yet coming, the devil jerks Nathan from my grasp, throws him down, and tears him again.

Will this agony never end for my son? For his mother? For me?

How long can I watch the only child of my heart be torn asunder? How am I to bear it?

Nathan lies on the ground, his limbs flailing, as he foams and gnashes his teeth. I can no longer keep my tears from falling. How could any father not weep at the sight of his son--his precious only son--in such a state?

With His eyes still upon my child and His voice gentle with compassion, Jesus asks me, "How long is it ago since this came unto him?"

And I answer, "Of a child." The memories flood my mind and heart. The demon took him when he was small, just starting to call his mother, *ma-ma*. That was his first--and only--spoken word. He has uttered none since. "And ofttimes it hath cast him into the fire, and into the waters, to destroy him."

My son throws his limbs about, as he did when the apostles tried to cast out the demons.

Roughly, I wipe my sleeve across my tear-streaked face. My voice is ragged with emotion as I raise my eyes to the Master. "But if thou canst do anything, have compassion on us, and help us."

"If thou canst believe." Jesus speaks softly and yet the words pierce their way into my heart. "All things are possible to him that believeth."

"*Lord, I believe!*" I believed when I first came to the apostles, but now my faith has faltered. If Nathan's healing depends upon mine own faith and not just the powers of the Healer, then is my faith sufficient? Did I not doubt after the apostles failed?

I bow my head in my shame as the tears well up again, and this time I let them fall freely as I cry out in my anguish, "*Help thou mine unbelief.*"

When I look again, Jesus gazes into my eyes and nods slightly. His face still glows. And, as I gaze into His eyes, I am filled with love, which pours into my body even as my tears flow out. Peace fills me, and I know with certainty He has the power to heal my Nathan.

How could I have doubted the Master?

The crowd closes in, more people running toward us. Jesus looks at them, and then back at my son.

Then Jesus rebukes the foul spirit, commanding thus: "*I charge thee, come out of him, and enter no more into him.*"

And the spirit cries and rends my son sore.

Has my faith not been sufficient? I would take this devil upon myself if only my son would suffer no more.

I see the instant the spirit leaves Nathan, and my son lies on the ground as one dead.

I cannot move in my fear. Has the spirit killed my son before it departed?

Many in the crowd wonder this, also, as I hear echoes of my own concern.

"He is dead." A man states flatly.

"Look, the child has passed on." This other man seems more compassionate in his tone.

A Father's Plea

A woman wails in mourning. "The boy is gone."

But Jesus ignores them all. He calmly leans over and takes my little son by the hand, and lifts him up--and Nathan does arise!

My heart overflows with joy and gratitude.

Even the usually argumentative and overly skeptical scribes and lawyers fall silent. All are amazed at the mighty power of God manifest in my son at this moment.

Nathan. He is a gift anew from God.

When my son looks into the eyes of Jesus and smiles, I weep with joy.

The Healer, still holding my son's hand, delivers Nathan to me, whole as he once was, and places my son's hand in mine.

It is my son, healed and whole and free of the spirit that has plagued him for so many years! My son is cured from this hour--from nearly the very *moment*--when Jesus commanded it to be so.

And when our three hands touch, Jesus looks again into my eyes, and I am also changed, healed as was my son, for the anguish of the past years washes away completely, pushed out by the love that floods into every corner of my heart. The light with which He shines is love, and I feel it in every fiber of my being.

"Thank you." I am barely able to choke out my words past my tears.

Jesus pats our hands, my son's and mine, then places His hand on my son's shoulder.

Finally I am able to look away from the Master.

Nathan smiles at me, and attempts to speak. The word comes out raspy and unsure, as he has not spoken in such a long time, and never learned to speak as other children, but I recognize the word, and it is the most beautiful sound in the world.

My boy calls me, "*Papa.*"

I drop to my knees again, and wrap my arms around my son, who has been restored to me, and he hugs me tightly. The Master smiles and steps away.

Finally, we pull back and laugh with joy.

"I think," I say, "that we should go find your mother."

Nathan nods at me. I stand and we begin our walk home, hand in hand, father and son.

I look back once to see the Master, His face still glowing, surrounded by the crowd.

When we reach our street, Nathan and I walk into our home, and Nathan calls out, "Ma-ma."

I will never forget the look of joy on my wife's face, as she, too, is healed.

Master, who did sin,
this man,
or his parents,
that he was born blind?

(John 9:2)

EYES TO SEE
Blind Man Healed on the Sabbath

I sit often on the street leading to the great temple, my cup before me for others to throw in their coins. I depend on the generosity of others, for I am blind, and have been since my birth.

My mother says my smile brightens her heart and my eyes are as blue as the sky. Her voice tells me that blue is good and beautiful, but I know not what else this color is.

Thus I have beautiful eyes with which I cannot see. My hands and ears and skin must act in place of my eyes.

With my fingers, I know my mother's face, the slight wrinkles around her eyes, her smile.

With my sensitive skin and sense of smell, I know if it will rain, something others seem not to sense.

With my ears, I recognize my father's footsteps--and those of many other people I know. I can tell people from the smallest sounds they make, sounds sighted people seem not even to notice. Such things as yawns. Coughs. Clearing of throats. Even their breathing reveals them.

And I have an ability to hear truth when it is spoken--and likewise the absence of truth--merely by hearing a person's voice and their words. I have been able to do thus since I was a child.

I have spent my life listening. When young, I listened to the other children laugh and run and play while I sat to the side and helped my mother with her simplest tasks. I listened to everything, and learned much of people.

I still sit along the side while others go about their business. Though blind, yet am I now a man, and must bring in money to help with household expenses. Thus I sit, in the road, cup before me. Always listening intently.

Most days, I raise my voice and call out to others for mercy when I hear them approach, to entice them to toss me a coin or two. But I not thus on this, the holy Sabbath. I feel pensive, expectant, as if something comes my way and I know not what. But the air fairly crackles with it, as when a storm approaches, and yet not the same at all.

I listen to the voices swirling around me. Men. Women. Children. Their words flow over me, as though these people bring fragments of conversation, like pieces of their lives, to throw into my cup.

I know many of them and many greet me.

But one group of men's voices I do not recognize. A large group, maybe ten men? Fifteen? More? I am not sure. But I hear the friendship between them.

They stop before me and pause.

I wait for I know not what.

One of the men asks, "Jesus, Master, who did sin, this man, or his parents, that he was born blind?"

Ah. *This* question. How many times, I wonder, have I been asked what was my sin that I was born blind. Many times have I pondered this question.

But always I come back to this further question: What could possibly be my sin as a mere babe within the womb? Did I kick too hard perhaps?

My thoughts are cynical, I suppose, but I understand not how I could have sinned. Since my birth, yes, of course, as have we all. But within the womb? And my parents are goodly folk who seek to keep the Law, so what was their sin? Is there no other explanation for blindness?

I was taught by my parents of a life before this one and a life that continues afterward. And it is during this life before that I am said to have sinned. I cannot believe that; no matter how many men repeat it to me.

Certainly none of the explanations I have ever been given have rung true in my ears. And I wonder what the answer this day will be from this Master.

The Master answers. *"Neither hath this man sinned, nor his parents."*

A shiver of truth runs through my body, as though I have tasted something incredibly and unexpectedly sweet. The man's voice brings me great comfort, one man's voice amongst the many others who *do* consider me a sinner.

But what a voice! Melodious and low pitched, it radiates love and compassion, and my heart tells me thus: *The man speaks true. I have not sinned. Neither have my parents sinned.* But I also wonder, if none of us did sin, why then am I blind?

As though he hears my very thoughts, the Master continues. "But that the works of God should be made manifest through him."

Through me? Through my blindness? The works of God made manifest? This intrigues me, and I wait again to hear the answer of this Master whose words bring peace to my soul, whose truth calms my heart. Is this man a prophet, then, that he knows such things?

"I must work the works of Him that sent me, while it is day; the night cometh, when no man can work." When the Master's voice comes again, it feels as if he is saying other words. *I am with you. The time cometh when I shall have finished my work, then I go unto the Father.* I know not where I hear those words, but they burn themselves into my bosom.

"As long as I am in the world, I am the light of the world."

Light is something I know not. My world is darkness. Oppressive, heavy, overwhelming darkness. Not even a glimmer of light shines upon me. When I feel the sun warming my body, I imagine this must be what light *feels* like.

I have heard that light conquers darkness. The sun conquers the dark of the night. A candle conquers the darkness of a room.

If this Master truly is the light of the world, then can he conquer also *my* darkness? Hope that has never lived before in my heart now flutters there.

I hear a man spit upon the ground, and then the Master explains to me that he is making clay from the spittle, and is going to anoint mine eyes with the clay.

When his hands touch my face--a gesture I make often to 'see' but others have no need for--a warmth as of the sun flows through me.

Then the Master puts his hand upon my shoulder, and says, "Go, wash in the pool of Siloam."

The words are a command and I feel somehow compelled to obey. I *will* obey. I stand.

Anointed clay can serve only one purpose--to heal. And the act Jesus requires of me will test my faith before that healing.

No one has offered me hope of a cure before. No one has ever heard of blindness being cured.

I leave these men, who continue on their journey, and I make my way to the pool of Siloam. I move more quickly than usual, excitement growing within me, but still more slowly than those with sight. My hand brushes the buildings as I walk, showing me the way as others are shown by their eyes.

As I wade into the pool, I do not take time even to remove the sandals from my feet or to walk out farther, but drop to my knees so as to bring my face closer to the water as quickly as I can.

I splash the water from the pool onto my eyes, and wash the clay from my eyes. I use my tunic to wipe the water from my eyelids.

And then I open my eyes--to a world unlike anything I have ever experienced.

Everything is so bright!

Everything has been transformed.

Darkness into light. Color. *Sight.*

Glorious sunlight shines through the clouds and reflects from the surface of the pool.

I have tried to imagine colors, but now realize how miserably I failed in my attempts.

The blue of the sky that my mother has tried to describe to me is glorious.

Trees, I have been told, are green--and thus I now know green is a lush and living color, almost glowing in its radiance. Individual leaves flutter and twist in the breeze. I touch the leaves to know with a surety that, yes, this is a tree.

A bird flies overhead and I know not what color it is, but the flight takes my breath away with its beauty.

Others have told me the ground beneath my sandals is brown. As I take a stumbling step from the pool, I see this brown.

And I understand, for the first time what shades of colors are, for my sandals are another shade of brown, and yet another are my arms and legs.

And my hands! I hold them before my face, in wonder, and watch how the veins bulge. I am surprised hands are not as beautiful as I imagined--but to *see* them is glorious.

I see people--milling around, walking, talking, seeing--*as do I!*

I see!

Tears spring to my eyes, my eyes that now see everything, in such vividness I am nearly overwhelmed by the blessing of sight. Gratitude spills from my heart to Jesus, who has given me this gift.

I still gauge my route by my old way of counting the number of my steps and streets and where to turn, listening to the sounds and taking note of the smells, but I run where before I would have walked cautiously with my fingers touching the gates of the homes.

As I approach my home, I see several people. I know them not by name, until a large older man speaks, and I recognize my neighbor, Samuel. "Can runnest thou so quickly? Are you not afraid you will fall?"

"Oh, dear friend, I see!"

Samuel cries out, and other neighbors join him, astounded.

"Is not this he that sat and begged?" asks Nissim, the butcher.

"This *is* he." The excited voice belongs to Taavi, my mother's dear friend. She is sobbing in wonderment.

Yet another man claims, "He is *like* him." His voice is filled with disbelief.

I laugh and say, "I *am* he. The one who sat and begged. The one who was blind from birth."

Samuel shakes his head in wonder. "How were thine eyes opened?" He is happy for me, I can hear it.

I answer joyously, "A man that is called Jesus made clay and anointed mine eyes, and said unto me, 'Go to the pool of Siloam, and wash.' I went and washed; and I received sight."

Then the crowd around me asks, "Where is he?"

"I know not," I answer, wishing I did know so I could thank him for his wondrous gift to me.

The crowd, still incredulous and murmuring, takes me--who was blind--into the outer court of the temple, a marvelous sight.

When I am brought before the Pharisees, they also ask me how I received my sight.

Again I tell the glorious story. "The man called Jesus put clay upon mine eyes, and I washed, and do see."

Therefore says one of the Pharisees, a tall angry man named Efrat, "This man is not of God, because he keepeth not the Sabbath Day."

Another disagrees. "How can a man that is a sinner do such miracles?"

And thus there is a division among them.

I know they argue now not of *my* sin, but of what they consider the sin of this Jesus, who healed me. The voices of those who, like this Efrat, believe Jesus is a sinner, are filled with such anger and hatred toward the man Jesus that I marvel.

Just as these men once questioned whose sin had caused my blindness, now they dispute whose sin has taken away my blindness.

Then the first Pharisee, Efrat, says to me again, "What sayest thou of him who hath opened thine eyes?"

I remember my earlier thought, and as I say it aloud, I know the truth of it. "He is a prophet."

But the Jews do not believe concerning me, that I was blind, and received my sight, and so they call for my parents. Cannot they see for themselves? They have passed me upon the streets, begging, and now they watch me come forth seeing.

I am moved to the back of the room, into an antechamber. But as soon as the older couple enter the room, I know it is them. Though I have never seen them before with my eyes, my ears recognize their steps and my heart warms within my bosom.

My mother is beautiful! Her hair is dark and full and her face is lovely. My father looks strong and healthy, and now I know what honor and character look like on a face for I know my father, and beauty for I know my mother.

When my parents catch sight of me, and realize I can see them, they are astounded. The crowd and Taavi have undoubtedly told them already, but hearing and seeing are two different things, I now know.

Tears course down my cheeks, and my parents weep with me from across the room.

The Pharisees ask my parents, saying, "Is this your son, who ye saw was born blind?"

"Yes, this is my son," my father announces proudly, "who was born blind."

My mother nods and touches her hand to her mouth, overcome.

The Pharisees ask, "How then doth he now see?"

And my parents answer them and say, "We know that this is our son, and that he was born blind. But by what means he now seeth, we know not; or who hath opened his eyes, we know not. He is of age. Ask him. He shall speak for himself."

These words my parents speak because they fear the rulers of the Jews, for we have all heard that these men have agreed already that if any man does confess he is Christ, that man should be put out of the synagogue. They are also wary that we are being questioned thus in this place. Therefore say my parents, 'He is of age. Ask him.'

I wonder if these men think Jesus is the Christ. Has he said he is? Do my parents believe that only the Christ could have opened mine eyes?

Again the Pharisees call me back to the front of the room. "Give God the praise. We know that this man is a sinner."

We are all sinners, comes the thought to my mind, but I remember the voice of this man Jesus and how it was filled with truth. Does a prophet sin? I shrug. "Whether he is a sinner or no, I know not. One thing I know, that, whereas I was blind, now I see."

92

Then say they to me again, "What did he do to thee? How opened he thine eyes?"

I weary of these questions with which they try to steal away the joy of my new sight. And so I answer them, "I have told you already, and ye did not hear or believe; wherefore would ye hear it again?" Perhaps I should not have said the next words, but the lies and hatred I hear in the voices of these men who would be my spiritual leaders anger me. "Will ye also be his disciples?"

I hear gasps of indignation and self-righteousness, as fury distorts their faces and I now know what ugliness looks like. They revile me, saying, "*Thou* art his disciple, but we are *Moses'* disciples. We know that God spake unto Moses. As for this fellow, we know not from whence he is."

The truth rises within me and will not be stopped. "Why herein is a marvelous thing, that ye know not from whence he is, and yet he hath opened mine eyes. Now we know that God heareth not sinners: but if any man be a worshiper of God, and doeth His will, him He heareth. Since the world began was it not heard that any man opened the eyes of one that was born blind." I point to my eyes that were blind and now see, and look them each in their eyes that refuse to see. "If this man were not of God, he could do nothing."

Furious at my words, they say unto me, "Thou wast altogether born in sins, and dost thou teach us?"

Again I know the lies, for in my mind I hear again the voice of truth, the Master's voice: *Neither hath this man sinned, nor his parents.*

And they who had called for me now cast me out.

From the synagogue. From the temple. From my former life. For being healed, they excommunicate me? What sin is it to be healed?

My heart is heavy. My parents will sorrow greatly.

I go back through the town toward my home, still followed by a noisy, marveling crowd. A group of men approach me. I know them not by sight, but when one speaks, I recognize the voice of the Master--the One who healed my eyes. Thankfulness wells up within me and spills from my lips.

"Dost thou believe on the Son of God?" he asks.

I answer and say, "Who is He, Lord, that I might believe in Him?"

And Jesus, the Master, says unto me in His voice of truth, "Thou hast both seen Him, and it is He that talkest with thee."

I look into His eyes, and I see the truth of God. "Lord, I believe."

Then I worship the Son of God, the One who has healed me. Now I know He is truly of God, not merely a prophet, but God's own Son. And God's Son must needs be the Messiah. Truly He is the Christ.

But why would the followers of God who rule in the temple fear and hate the Christ who was prophesied by Isaiah, by Abraham, by the very Moses of whom they claim to be disciples?

Jesus smiles at me and there is all beauty and truth in His face. Then He turns to the others who are with me, for many have followed me, still astounded at my new sight. "For judgment I am come into this world, that they which see *not* might see; and that they which see might be made blind."

Some of the Pharisees which are with us hear these words, and they mutter. One says unto him, "Are we blind also?" The voice says he is highly offended and his face also reflects this.

Jesus says unto them, "If ye were blind, ye should have no sin: but now ye say, 'We see;' therefore, your sin remaineth."

Before I was a Jew who was blind from birth. Now I am no longer a Jew, but I can see clearly. Joy fills my heart. *I have met the Son of God this day and He has healed me.*

I can see. I did not sin.

Though my life will change from being cast from the presence of the Pharisees from the temple, I will no longer have to listen to their lies for I see clearly that they have perverted the true way.

They hate and would cast out the very Christ. I heard it in their voices. I saw it in their faces. I felt it in my heart.

I was blind, and now I see.

The Christ is here.

Hallelujah. I have been cast out, but my joy is full.

And Jesus answering said,
'Were there not ten cleansed?
But where are the nine?'

(Luke 17:17)

THIS STRANGER
Leper Who Gives Thanks

I stand in the brush, off the main path, waiting for a man with the power to heal me.

I am today one of a group of ten. We are of the ones who must, by law, always stand afar off from normal, healthy people. Who must stay apart. Who must cry out, *"Unclean,"* when any approach or we walk through the city so none will without knowing come close enough to catch our disease. Ten who have no hope of a normal life.

I am Caleb. With me are six other men, Eben, Jared, Micah, Oren, Reuben, and Thaddeus, and three women, Etel, Mava, and Anat. Our names stand for wonderful things. *Bold. Rock. Descending. Gift from God. Tree. Behold a son. Wise. Noble. Pleasant. Singer.* Many good and marvelous things that we no longer are.

97

I share our old names for they are all we have left. Our former lives are in tatters, as are our rent garments and even our flesh.

We have new names now, spoken in a hiss.

Unclean Ones.

Hideous Abominations.

Lepers.

Our ailments, though not all the same, have one commonality. We all have ailments of the skin. Some have the white leprosy, their flesh intact but marked by flowers of white blossoming and growing. Others have hard scaly rashes.

Mava, Thaddeus, and I have the worst of the ailments--the living death. We have lost the feeling in our very bodies. Without pain to warn us, we harm ourselves. The very flesh rots and falls from our bones.

Our fingers are blackened and shortened and what is left is twisted into claws. Our noses are sunken into our faces. My eyes are cloudy and painful and I see more dimly now than before, and if my eyes are as hideous to gaze upon as Mava's, then I am glad I cannot look upon my own face.

The normal ones do not usually look upon us. Occasionally, small children--not having yet learned-- will gaze upon us from afar and cry out in terror, and their mothers must pull them close to comfort them and warn them to stay far, far away from such as us.

I may feel no pain in my body, but there is great pain in the heart of this unclean one. No one wants to look at me. No one has touched me in years, besides occasionally the other lepers. I yearn for human contact, simple comfort, but I find none for such as me.

Now that I am a leper, the fact that I am a Samaritan no longer seems to bother anyone. Being a leper is so much worse. It is as if the Samaritan part of me lay on top of my skin, and now it has fallen away with the flesh.

Only my fellow lepers do sometimes remember, at those times when they need to feel better than someone else. Then they call to mind my difference from them and it makes them feel superior to me, a stranger in their land. But mostly they forget I am Samaritan and we remember only that we are fellow lepers, who must stand together, while afar off, and we are superior to no one.

We stand together thus today, waiting, watching.

Jesus of Nazareth will be here soon. Word has come from Capernaum, from Ephraim by the wilderness, from Galilee and Samaria.

It has been rumored that Jesus, who brought Lazarus back to life after he lay in the tomb for four days, is coming to our village. Jesus has raised three people from the dead. The daughter of Jairus was raised within an hour of her death, the widow's son in Nain within the same day as his body had been prepared and was being carried toward the grave, but Lazarus was already in the tomb *four days*. Every Jew of my day knows that in the fourth day, the spirit departs from the area where lies the body, and the decomposition of the corpse may proceed unhindered.

Surely one with the great power and authority needed to raise a man from death unto life--even a man whose flesh had begun to rot in the tomb--can surely also heal a man whose flesh falls from his bones while he yet breathes and hobbles around.

Surely he can heal *me*.

As we wait, I ponder the things I have heard of this Jesus and of Lazarus. Though we lepers stand afar off, we overheard the excited voice of the man called Malak, who told the tale of Lazarus.

He had been in Bethany, nigh unto Jerusalem, accompanied by Jews antagonistic to Jesus. When Jesus arrived in Bethany, on the fourth day, Martha (who is a sister of Lazarus) met Him and said, "Lord, if thou hadst been here, my brother had not died. But I know that, even now, whatsoever thou wilt ask of God, God will give it thee."

Jesus had answered, saying, "Thy brother shall rise again."

"I know that he shall rise again in the resurrection at the last day."

And Jesus had said unto her, "I *am* the resurrection, and the life. He that believeth in me, though he were dead, yet shall he live. And whomsoever liveth and believeth in me shall *never* die. Believest thou this?"

"Yea, Lord. I believe that thou art the Christ, the Son of God, which should come into the world."

And Malak had told the crowd that Martha went her way, and her sister Mary came next to Jesus and, using the very words of Martha, mournfully said, "Lord, if thou hadst been here, my brother had not died."

When Jesus saw her weeping, He groaned in spirit and was troubled, and said, "Where have ye laid him?"

They said unto him, "Come and see."

And then, Malak said, Jesus wept, and the Jews said, "Behold how Jesus loved Lazarus!" Malak, himself, marveled at the tears of Jesus, and I, listening, also.

And some of them said, "Could not this man, which opened the eyes of the blind, have caused that even this man should not have died?"

Jesus again groaned as He came to the grave, which was a cave, and a stone lay upon it. He said, "Take ye away the stone."

Martha, the sister of him that was dead, said, "Lord, by this time Lazarus stinketh, for he hath been dead four days."

"Said I not unto thee, that, if thou wouldest believe, thou shouldest see the glory of God?"

Then they took away the stone from the place where the dead was laid. And Jesus lifted up His eyes, and said, "Father, I thank thee that thou hast heard me. And I knew that thou hearest me always, but because of the people which stand by I said it, that they may believe that thou hast sent me."

And, then, Jesus cried forth with a loud voice: *"Lazarus, come forth!"*

And Malak had practically shouted the next part: *And Lazarus did obey and came forth!* He walked from the tomb, and even those of Malak's friends who were antagonistic to Jesus could not claim it false.

And because Jesus raised Lazarus after his spirit left his body and his body had begun to rot, the rulers are incensed, and it is also rumored that they now seek the life of Jesus. For the raising of Lazarus is on the lips of all. *Jesus raised Lazarus from the very tomb after four days!* This is the whisper blowing across the land.

It has even blown to this far corner where I exist in my not-alive-and-yet-not-dead state.

After raising Lazarus, Jesus therefore walked no more openly among the Jews. No one knew where He had gone for a time, but now the rumors again fly. He had gone thence unto a country near to the wilderness, to a city called Ephraim, with his disciples.

That is not far from our village. And the whisper today is that He is traveling our way. The whispers even invade the camp of the Unclean Ones, for those speaking are excited, even as Malak, at the news.

Beside me, Mava raises a hideous hand to point. "Look. Someone comes. Who is it?"

She can only see shapes and shadows but still has seen first.

And, afar off, I see a group of men walking.

We talk among ourselves excitedly and then grow quiet as we watch the group of men. But, more, we study the man who leads them.

Is this Jesus of Nazareth? Is this the healer of the dead? *Is this the healer of the living dead, healer of the lepers? Can He heal me?*

My hope burns high, and I lift my voice. "Jesus, Master, have mercy on us."

At the sound of my voice, my fellow sufferers cry out, as well. "Have mercy on us, Master."

When Jesus sees us, He stops. Across the field that lies between us, He looks at us for a moment in silence.

Did you understand my words? *He looks at us!*

Not as a child, who screams in terror. Not as an adult, whose face grimaces in revulsion. Not as an old woman who mutters and scurries away. Not even as another leper, for we also find it difficult to look sometimes.

No, He looks directly into each of our eyes, one by one, acknowledging us as *people,* and people who are not unclean. There is not a look of revulsion upon His face, but one of loving compassion. When He looks into my ailing eyes, a warmth runs through my body and a peace through my heart such as I have never known, even when I was whole of body.

"Go show yourselves," He says unto us with mercy, "unto the priests."

As if that were all it would take. To show ourselves unto the priests. *As if we are already healed and have need of an offering of two doves to cleanse us from our time of uncleanness.* Even healed, we still must present ourselves before the priests so they can pronounce us clean. Only then can we go among society again.

The man's voice resonates with power, and I take a step toward the synagogue. I *will* show myself unto the priests. I *will* obey. I *will* be healed.

I look down at my arms. My fingers are still blackened and stubbed, but that does not matter. For the healer has spoken and thus I am healed already! It has taken years for my body to fall to its ruin, and I know not how long healing will take. But I *am* healed. And I will show myself to the priests that they may see my healing. And I *will* be healed, though I know not how.

All Jesus had to do to bring Lazarus forth from the tomb was to command him: "Lazarus, come forth!" And now Jesus has commanded us to go show ourselves unto the priests. I, like Lazarus, will obey.

"Come, let us go," I urge the others. And ten of us unclean ones walk toward the synagogue, calling out "*Unclean!*" to warn the others, walking and hoping.

And it comes to pass that, as we go, we are cleansed. In an instant, a warmth such as that I felt when I looked into the eyes of Jesus flows through me, like living, healing water flowing through my limbs--and I am healed!

My arms are whole. My fingers are long and slender again, a healthy brown color I scarce remember.

I touch my face. *I feel it!*

My shoulders. My legs. There is sensation again throughout my limbs. And I can see clearly!

I am cleansed. I do now truly have need of a priest to make an offering for uncleanness.

I look at the others, who have also discovered their healing. We dance in the street and hug each other. Then the others run toward the synagogue, the priests.

But I hesitate. When I see that I am healed, I am overcome. The warmth in my heart remains and I am overwhelmed with thankfulness. Tears well in my now-healthy eyes and roll down my now-smooth cheeks as I walk back on my now-strong feet toward Jesus, The Healer of All, and with a loud voice I glorify God.

When I reach Jesus, I fall on my face at His feet, giving Him thanks, though I am but a Samaritan, and thus a stranger in this land.

And Jesus looks into my eyes and smiles.

The warmth spreads and I feel a new healing within me, as the older wounds of being rebuffed as a Samaritan drain from my heart.

"Were there not ten cleansed?" Jesus asks. "But where are the nine? There are not found any that returned to give glory to God," He looks at me again and says gently, "save this stranger."

He touches my shoulder--*Another person's touch! Yet another gift from the Master!*--and says unto me, "Arise, go thy way; thy faith hath made thee whole."

And again I obey. I rise from my knees and, with one glance back at the Master, I do as He says and make my way toward the synagogue, the priest, and the clean new life He has given me.

My heart is full of joy, my breast is warm with it, and even the air I breath is suffused with it.

At last, this stranger has found a home.

Judas, one of the twelve,
went before them,
and drew near unto Jesus
to kiss Him.

But Jesus said unto him,
Judas, betrayest thou
the Son of Man
with a kiss?

(Luke 22:47-48)

THIRTY PIECES OF SILVER
Judas Iscariot

It is done.

I have wearied of watching my Lord and Master hesitate to take His place among men.

I have seen the miracles. The healing of the blind, the lame, the leprous. Even the very raising of the dead from the tomb, after four days, when the spirit had already passed over the threshold from this world to the next.

Thus I know Jesus has power to save Himself.

And by so doing He will be forced to take His place.

Ruler of the Israelites. Savior of His people. King of the Jews--even as His earthly father, Joseph, would have been King of the Jews had he lived and had not the Romans conquered.

Even the Messiah, prophesied by all the prophets throughout all generations of time, from Father Abraham to Moses to Isaiah.

I can see it now. Jesus will lead a great triumphant army against the Romans. The Jews will never have to walk a mile carrying a Roman soldier's belongings again. Never again the *second* mile.

We will drive them from this place.

And Jesus will rule, from the Sea of Galilee to the Great Sea, from Sidon to Judea. None will make afraid.

And I have brought it about.

He is far too humble, speaking of turning the other cheek and the meek inheriting the earth, and asking those healed to say nothing of Him.

Now Jesus will ascend His throne, as He was meant to do. And I will rise at His side.

So I walk tonight, happy, the weight of thirty pieces of silver heavy in my pouch. A good day's wages for helping put things right.

Walking behind me are officers sent from the chief priests and Pharisees--noisy men with loud, raucous laughter, coarse songs and shouts of ugliness--come thither with lanterns and torches and weapons. Ha. As if weapons can save them from the power of the Messiah.

As we reach the Garden of Gethsemane, I see my Master and the other apostles. My friends. My Lord glows with power, more than ever before. I feel it and exult in it. This is the power that will rule nations, with me by His side. Yes, I have made the right choice. Now *is* the time.

I stride to my friend and cannot hold back my words. "Master." I kiss Him much on the cheeks. I look into His eyes and am warmed by the love I see there for me. "*Master.*"

I feel the incredible power radiating from Him, as if this night He has somehow taken upon Himself the power of Elohim Himself. It *is* truly time for Him to overcome all.

As well as love in His eyes, I also see sadness. "Judas, betrayest thou the Son of Man with a kiss?"

He knows what I have done, but I have not betrayed Him, only helped move events as they need be for the greater good. To bring about His mission. When He has taken His throne, He will thank me.

Still, there is a part of me that grows afraid at what I have done.

I move to stand beside the soldiers. I want to see them try to take Him, for they cannot.

Jesus turns His quiet but intense focus onto the men behind me, who grow quiet. "Whom seek thou?"

They shout out, "Jesus of Nazareth."

Jesus says simply, "*I am He.*"

A physical wave of power rolls off my Master, pushing us back, driving us all to the ground.

They cannot take Him. I knew it. He will take His place now. My spirit exults in this knowledge. With the Messiah at the head of our armies, we cannot fail. Jesus can simply walk out of any trap--Roman or Jewish--as He has so many before. He will lead our armies to great victory. Jesus will save our people.

The Messiah is here.

Jesus asks again "Whom seek ye?" as if to remind the mob of why they have come.

And the men, picking themselves up carefully, repeat, more quietly now, "Jesus of Nazareth."

Jesus answers, "I have told you that I am He." It is as though He is goading the unruly men to their original action. Good. That is good. He means to take the opportunity before Him. "If therefore ye seek me, let these go their way, that the saying might be fulfilled, which He spake, of them which thou gavest me have I lost none."

Ever impetuous Peter draws forth his sword and slashes the ear from the servant of the high priest. Cannot Peter see this must be so? Has he no faith in Jesus' ability to free Himself?

Jesus rebukes Peter, saying, "Put up again thy sword into his place; for all they that take the sword shall perish with the sword. Thinkest thou that I cannot now pray to my Father, and He shall presently give me more than twelve legions of angels?"

I know He can call down legions of angels. And I hope He will pray for exactly that, as I watch Jesus perform a miracle before our very eyes, touching the servant's ear and healing him. Surely these men will be able to see, finally, whom it is they have taken.

But they are blind. They murmur against Him.

"Are you come out, as against a thief, with swords and staves for to take me?" Jesus motions toward the crowd with an upraised arm. "When I was daily with you in the temple, ye stretched forth no hands against me. But this is your hour, and the power of darkness."

He lowers His arm slowly. "The cup which my Father hath given me, shall I not drink it?"

The hour of darkness, yes--but also the hour of Christ's power.

And then they reach out to take Him. I wait--for Him to turn His power on them. For Him to resist. For Him to smite them with a touch. For Him to send them reeling backward, as He did before. But He does none of these things.

Instead, they lay their hands upon Him and take Him, and He allows it. The disciples run, even Peter. One young disciple, his linen cloth covering grabbed by the crowd, flees naked.

I follow after Jesus. I desire to see His moment of power. I ache to see Him in the instant He takes His place. I yearn to be at His side when they acknowledge Him--*King of the Jews!*

The night grows long. He is taken first to he who was high priest, Annas, and then to the son-in-law of Annas, Caiaphas, who is high priest this same year. I see Simon Peter following Jesus, as well; he dares not come into the room as I do, but hides in the shadows.

They question Jesus and He answers for awhile, then grows silent. They seek for men to give false witness against Him. Though many come forth, none are found with lies sufficient enough to use against Him, until finally two men say they heard Jesus claim He could destroy the temple and build another within three days. Yet even these two men do not agree together.

The night drags on, longer and longer, and Jesus is silent still to their questions. *Why will He not speak? Why does He not put an end to this mockery?*

Finally, the high priest--whose servant Jesus healed in the Garden--demands, "Art thou the Christ, the Son of the Blessed?"

At last!

"I am," Jesus states. "And ye shall see the Son of Man sitting on the right hand of power, and coming in the clouds of heaven."

The right hand of power. *This is the moment for which I have waited and planned.*

The high priest rends his clothes, and wails, "What need we any further witnesses? Ye have heard his blasphemy." He motions broadly to the priests and bellows. "What think ye?"

Blasphemy is punishable by death. Why will Jesus not take His place? Does He wait to make His escape more dramatic? I grow more nervous still.

Jesus turns His head and looks into my eyes. Again I feel His power and His love and His sadness--*all for me.*

Why sadness for me? I have helped Him. If He will only show them the power I know He has.

But He does not. They spit on Him and buffet Him and strike Him with the palms of their hands. They mock Him and tell Him to *prophesy.* They humiliate Him.

And still He does nothing.

If He does not stop them, what will happen?

Outside, I hear a cock crow. It is morning, and still Jesus does not free Himself. The cock crows twice. Thrice.

And, now, they have condemned Him in a mockery of a trial, for they have broken every rule and told every lie. If Jesus of Nazareth does not soon show His power, I know what these evil men will do next. They will take Him to Pilate and have Him put to death. But surely He will not let that happen. Surely He will not let these men end His life.

Yet they have condemned Him by trial. He *has* let it happen. They have condemned Him and they drag Him away, now to take Him before Pilate and have His life taken from Him. He can now show His power to Rome itself.

But then I look into Christ's eyes once more. And I see He will not save Himself. He can. But He will not.

His words come back to haunt me. When He spoke of His Kingdom, He did not mean He would ascend to the throne of Israel and lead the rebellion against Rome.

Now I understand and my heart goes cold.

What have I done?

I have allowed myself to be deceived. I have believed the lies of the evil one, who has taken the truth and twisted it into a form that enticed me to believe, who has taken my discontent and impatience and used it to destroy all. Who led me to believe that Jesus needed my help. The evil one used my greed--I

113

recognize it now for what it is--to bring down my Master.

In horror, I stumble from the room. Outside, I see Peter, fallen on his face and weeping bitterly.

But Peter's bitterness can be nothing next to the icy pain that permeates my very soul, burrows into every part of me and eats at me like worms.

Frantic, I hope to excuse myself. He could have shown His power. He could have overcome them. He could have taken His place. *Why will He not?*

But my thoughts cannot stop the horrible truth from entering into my heart.

I have betrayed Jesus unto death. *I* have betrayed the Son of God. *I* have betrayed the Messiah.

With a kiss have I betrayed Him!

I have betrayed the One who came to rule, to bind all wounds, with love for all. Him have I betrayed.

I have betrayed the very Son of God.

When He spoke of one last night, at supper, He meant me! He knew then.

I am the betrayer!

I hurry to the temple, where I find the chief priests and elders, laughing and exulting in their victory over Jesus, making merry and rejoicing, drinking and dancing.

In my trembling hands, I clutch the pouch which holds the thirty pieces of silver. Thirty pieces of silver meant to prod Jesus to take His rightful place. Thirty pieces of silver that have become the price of blood.

Thirty hideous reminders of what I have done. Thirty embers burning against my skin through the pouch.

"I have sinned," I say and my voice shakes with the knowledge of it, "in that I have betrayed the innocent blood."

I realize by the look in their eyes that they already know Jesus is innocent. I had thought these men who sought His life truly believed Him to be a blasphemer. But I see clearly in my moment of searing pain--these men know the truth. They have known it all along. They already know who Jesus is! And still they want Him dead.

And I--*the betrayer*--have given Him up into their hands.

"Innocent blood," I repeat. I will not keep this silver. I *cannot*.

The chief priest looks into my eyes, and there I see hatred and evil and lust for power.

The same lust for power I had earlier myself. The lust to see Jesus overthrow everything, even the Romans, and take His place so I could be at His side, at the side of power.

"What is that to us?" The chief priest laughs and motions me away. "See thou to it."

The men laugh harshly and loudly together.

One of the priests drinks of his wine. When he sets his cup roughly on the table, the wine spills over. He wipes his mouth with his sleeve and smiles harshly. "Thy sins be upon thee."

In the lamp light, the spilled wine glistens on the wooden table like dark drops of blood. *Innocent blood.*

I cannot bear it.

I throw down the pieces of silver in the temple, away from me, and depart. They cannot make me keep the payment.

Yet it does not take away the unbearable pain that wracks my soul, for I have betrayed my Lord and Master. I am sickened that I ever lusted after those coins.

As I stumble through the streets, my soul too anguished even for tears to flow, my heart bursts within me at the enormity of what I have done.

Jesus will not take His place. They will kill Him. And He will let them, though He has the power to stop it. I know not why, only that it is so.

It is done indeed. And I am to blame.

I untie my sash as I search for a tree.

I cannot live with what I have done. I cannot live if my Master is gone. I cannot face the other apostles. I can face no one, for all will know what I have done. *I* will know.

I cannot ask for forgiveness, for I have betrayed the Savior to His enemies, to those who hate Him and will see Him dead.

The Law of Moses demands an eye for an eye, a tooth for a tooth, a life for a life. And, giving up my life, perhaps I can escape the guilt and horror of having betrayed the Son of God.

Even knowing I betrayed Him, Jesus had love for me in His eyes. I remember with anguish both His love and His sadness. Now I understand.

I tie my sash around my neck and climb into the tree. I secure the other end to a strong limb, and throw myself off.

My pain continues with me from this earth into the next realm and gains strength as I leave my body behind. I cannot escape so easily.

And still I feel Christ's love for me.

Verily I say unto thee,
today shall thou be with me
in Paradise.

(Luke 23:43)

IT IS FINISHED
The Thief On The Cross

The Roman soldiers lead me from the fortress Antonia. After the darkness of the prison, I squint as I come into the early morning light. One other prisoner--Gestas--is brought forth with me.

A third man is already in the main hall, surrounded by Roman soldiers. The man wears a richly textured purple robe. I wonder at the robe, until I hear the soldiers call out, "Hail, King of the Jews!" as they mockingly bow the knee before him, and I see the reed in his hand as scepter and the vicious crown of thorns pushed into his scalp.

A soldier snatches the reed from the man's hand and hits him on the head with it, driving the thorns deeper into his scalp. The man does not cry out, but I hear his sharp intake of breath, and I see blood trickling down his face in lines drawn from the cruel, sharp points of the thorns.

Some of the soldiers spit upon him.

Inwardly I cringe at the cruelty of the Romans which will be turned against me soon enough. In my relief their attention is not on me, I wonder why Gestas and I are not being spit upon, as well. What has this man done?

And how have I found myself in this horror? Oh, that I could go back and change what I have done. That I could have evaded the Roman patrol. But it is too late for that. I will be crucified. I am cursed. And I shall go to hell for my deeds.

As Gestas and I are shoved and stumble toward the bleeding man, another soldier reaches for the purple robe and rips it from his shoulders.

I gasp at the sight thus unveiled. I know not what this man has done, but he has already been punished for it. His back is torn and hanging in bleeding shreds of flesh.

Yet he does not cry out. I admire the man for his fortitude and his determination to stay silent before the hated Romans. I, too, am determined to remain silent.

I catch Gestas' eye and see his admiration for the man.

Are we next to be scourged? Many prisoners are scourged before being crucified, but not all. Many people die from the scourging alone. I shudder with the horror of the possibility. I have not been told what will happen to me this day.

Three soldiers bend, this time not in a mocking bow but so each may lift a titulus. The three signs proclaim our names and our crimes.

Printed upon my titulus, in Hebrew, Greek, and Latin so all may see me and read and know I am cursed, are the words: *This is Dysmas, a thief.* It says nothing of the noble Zealot cause for which I stole--to run the hated Romans from our land--for I have failed.

The titulus of Gestas also proclaims: *Thief.*

The soldier holding the third titulus turns and I read upon it the words: *This is Jesus of Nazareth, The King of the Jews.*

Is he truly then the King of the Jews? Why have I never heard of the man? Even if he were of the royal house of David, is that a crime? And if this is the King of the Jews, why is he here, in this place, being thus crucified? These people are deluded. Surely this is more mockery.

It is more likely that this Jesus is being killed for treason, for setting himself up as king and rebelling against Rome. My admiration for the man rises yet again.

The soldiers now give Jesus his own clothes back and the man winces as he dresses. The Romans care nothing for the nakedness of one walking to the cross, but it displeases the Jews to see nakedness except upon the cross, itself.

I do not want to hang upon the cross. I do not want to be cursed. I do not want to die this day.

But what of my wishes? We will all die soon enough, whether king or thief.

My heart pumps faster in my terror. What will they do to us? Knowing would make it easier. Or would it?

The Romans are very clever in the art of pain. At times they nail a *sedile*, a small seat, to the upright post, and the victim will then prolong his own agony by his desperate attempts to relieve that very agony. But I can at least take some hope in the knowledge that my death will not take days, for the Jews will insist our bodies be removed from the cross before the Sabbath, which begins at sunset.

And if I am not already dead by then, the Romans will break my legs, which will be incredibly painful, but will hasten my death. *Oh, that my death might be hastened. Dear God, if thou wilt answer the prayer of a cursed thief, please hasten my death!*

And then my body will be thrown onto the common grave. The Romans do not pray to our God, and know not the ways of civilized men, but only the barbarism and brutality of death and killing and torture beforehand. But the Jews will make sure it is not left on the cross as food for beasts and birds of prey.

I pull myself from these dark thoughts. They only serve to frighten me, and I will not give these Romans cause to doubt my courage, do what they may.

The Romans weary of their sport with the man Jesus and push the three of us toward our beams.

Jesus looks up and I see into his eyes and I am shocked at the power there. The man has been nearly killed by the scourging and yet he has such strength it amazes me. I feel it in the air between us. Then he looks away and I catch my breath again.

There are three of these patibulums lying on the ground. I struggle to heft this top beam which weighs over one hundred pounds and pushes down painfully upon my shoulders and back.

Gestas and Jesus also stand with their arms about their patibulums.

And we take the first step of the many that will take us the 650 yards from the fortress Antonia to the place of the skulls. The place of burial. Golgotha. Or, as the Romans call it, *Calvary.*

We are led following the Roman custom: a detail of hardened soldiers, led by one centurion, guarding their prisoners--two thieves and the King of the Jews.

We trudge along wearily, first Gestas, then Jesus, and finally myself.

A crowd follows, and many women wail for this Jesus. I cannot understand how he can carry this beam when it settles upon his torn back and shoulders.

Words come into my mind unbidden and long forgotten--the words of Isaiah which my father taught me as a small child. *I gave my back to the smiters, and my cheeks to them that plucked off the hair: I hid not my face from shame and spitting.*

What a strange memory to come to me in this moment. Again I watch Jesus struggle, and know that I could not walk this path if I had been scourged nearly to death before we began.

And indeed, after we have gone a hundred paces, Jesus stumbles, but rights himself and continues walking. But it is only another ten paces when he goes down. Still he does not cry out and my admiration rises for the man. I hope if I cannot be lucky and simply die, that I can be as stoic.

I stop, breathing hard with my own exertion and with my rising fear.

The centurion, impatient to get on with his grisly duty, points at a man passing by, and demands, "What is your name?"

"I am Simon from Cyrene," the man answers, his eyes wide. The man is large and strong, and that is doubtless why the centurion has chosen him.

The centurion now points at Jesus, struggling to rise, the beam still upon his shoulders. "Carry this man's patibulum to Calvary."

And because no one dares say nay to a Roman, especially a centurion, the man picks up the beam. Easily. *Ah, my friend, at least you get to put it down again and walk away. Would that I were carrying someone else's cross and not my own.*

Even with the beam on his shoulder, Simon the Cyrenian helps Jesus to his feet. The man must have the strength of three men!

The soldiers shove Jesus and he struggles to walk even without the beam's oppressive weight. Simon takes his place behind Jesus and before me.

A great company of people, including many women, follow us and throng us from all sides. They bewail and lament Jesus.

No one is here to mourn my death. Who is this Jesus that so many care for him?

Though it seems as though Jesus would not have strength to speak, he says unto the women, "Daughters of Jerusalem, weep not for me, but weep for yourselves, and for your children. For, behold, the days are coming, in the which they shall say, 'Blessed are the barren, and the wombs that never bare, and the paps which never gave suck.' Then shall they begin to say to the mountains, 'Fall on us,' and to the hills, 'Cover us.' For if they do these things in a green tree, what shall be done in the dry?"

I understand not his words to the women, but I am amazed at the strength in his voice.

We are nearly there now. I can see the upright posts affixed into the ground along the road, and my heart trembles within my breast. I force my face to show no expression, but fear seeps into my limbs and steals my breath.

The Romans lead us to a place where we can be displayed prominently so we may serve as a deterrent. Against what, I wonder? My sin is that I desire to be free of Roman rule, as does Gestas. And Jesus is either the King of the Jews--what sin is that?--or the most treasonous of the three of us.

But treason is punishable by a horrible death. And thus we are led to Golgotha. Dreaded Calvary. The place of the skulls and burial and the three stipes permanently affixed in place, awaiting one such as I to carry my beam to be hung thereon.

Another scripture slips into my mind. *But he was wounded for our transgressions, he was bruised for our iniquities: the chastisement of our peace was upon him; and with his stripes we are healed.* More words of Isaiah that I have not remembered for many, many years.

The Romans push back the crowd. Indeed, the women who have followed Jesus shrink back in horror from the violence that is to come and hold their distance. I hear their wails and try to imagine that some are also mourning my death, though that is not true.

Simon and Gestas and I drop the beams to the earth. And now, though Simon is free to go as I am not, he steps nearer the women, but stays to watch. Out of morbid curiosity? Or does he also wonder about this Jesus for whom he carried a cross?

A Roman brings me a cup filled with posca, the cheap, sour wine which the legionnaires favor, mingled with substances that help deaden the pain. I know this is not something the Romans do of their own accord, for they are everlastingly brutal, but it is to soothe the sensibilities of the Jews. And, as it is also to dull the pain, I drink as much as I can before the soldier pulls the cup from me.

I close my eyes and hope for the dulling of my senses to be quick. I have no wounds like those of Jesus. If I were he, I would need a whole bottle to deaden the pain.

But when I open my eyes, I see Jesus taste the drink and then, as if realizing what it is and what it will do, he does not drink of it more. I am amazed. I wish I could drink his portion, if he does not want it.

Perhaps he is so far gone with pain already that he is not thinking clearly.

A Psalm of David slips into my mind. *They gave me also gall for my meat; and in my thirst they gave me vinegar to drink.*

I have not thought of the scriptures for a long time, but my father told them to me as bedtime stories and explained to me that gall was tea mixed with either myrrh or hemlock. Either way I will begin to feel a numbness, but if there is hemlock, the numbness will not stop until I am dead. Mercifully. I hope for hemlock.

These scriptures that continue to sound within my mind are about . . . the *Messiah*. Why would they come thus into my head? Who is this Jesus?

I look around me in my last few moments of freedom before my horrible death. It is in the third hour, with the sun still low in the sky.

The soldiers make us shed our clothes so that we stand naked before them. And thus begins the real humiliation. We will hang without clothing on a cross in clear view of all who pass by, with our feet not far from the ground so that any who wish to spit upon us may do so.

I begin to feel the effect of the drink. My senses dull. *Thank merciful heaven.*

127

The Romans now turn efficiently to the business at hand. They throw us to the ground so that they may secure our arms to the beam. The man Jesus must be in excruciating pain already, lying in the dirt with his torn back, but still he makes no sound.

My fear nearly stops my breath. It overwhelms me until I am drowning in it. I fight also to stay silent.

Gestas cries out and rages and wails, and I am sorry for the loss of his dignity before these hated Romans.

Two Romans pull my arms up to the beam and tie them there. They take pleasure in their roughness, and they tie the ropes so tight that my arms are already numbingly painful.

Then they place the titulus above my head and nail it to the beam. Each blow reverberates through my arms and body.

I hear laughter from the Romans around Jesus' beam and then the sound of metal striking metal, many more times than it has taken for my titulus to be secured. I turn my head to look, only to discover the hideous truth: the soldiers are nailing his very arms to the beam!

I wince at his pain while bile rises within my throat.

And again he makes no sound!

Who is this Jesus?

David in his Psalms said, *For dogs have compassed me: the assembly of the wicked have enclosed me: they pierced my hands and my feet.*

They will pierce the hands and feet of the Messiah. Could this be He?

The women wail in the background and the sound fills the air, as they mourn Jesus' pain and humiliation and impending death.

The soldiers lift Jesus first, and affix his beam to the top of the middle post, the weight of his body jolting against the nails. I see the pain on his face.

Still the man does not cry out.

Then the Romans raise the patibulum to which Gestas is tied and drag him to the upright stile on the left. As the Romans lift and then drop the top beam into place, Gestas screams in pain.

They move me to put me on the right side of Jesus. When they lift the beam, the weight of my body pulls terribly on my arms. My shoulders and wrists and elbows all feel the strain, and I would not be surprised if they pulled loose from their place. I pant to keep the pain in check.

And when the beam drops into the notch on the stipes, my body thuds down and jerks up short, and even the drugged drink can not keep me from screaming in agony.

A soldier laughs at me. "That's nothing, thief. Wait until we nail your feet."

I shudder as they lift my feet to the post. And I bite my lips so that I may not scream again. And then the nails are driven into place.

The pain is excruciating.

The nerves break and the pain scatters through my legs until I think I will die.

Until I wish I *would* die.

Please let me be taken down from this cross!

And then begins the slow torture of crucifixion. I could never have imagined it would be this bad. And how much worse is it for Jesus, who has a torn back and has lost so much blood, and has his hands, his wrists, nailed to the cross, so that his arms must be filled with exquisite pain, as well as his feet and legs.

It is difficult to breathe. I twist. Searing cramps pull at my joints. And then I do what I said I would not do--I rest myself as best I can upon the *sedile* so my pain is lessened a bit. When I again hang down to ease the pain from my feet, the muscles in my arms seize.

And the worst of it is the struggle to draw breath. I have to push myself upward to breathe out, to cry out, to speak. And as I do, my full weight rests on the nails through my feet, and again there is searing agony up my legs.

And then I sink back to stop the agony in my feet and legs, and my arms cramp.

A terrible crushing pain begins deep in my chest.

I want to die! Please, God, may I die quickly!

From the side, I hear Gestas utter insults upon the onlookers. He is not the first on the cross to do so, and I realize now the reason he does is to seek relief from his own agony. I hope I do not succumb. I do not wish to give the Romans the pleasure of my pain.

And there is such pain as I never imagined.

The chief Jews gather below Jesus' cross. Through my pain, I again wonder, *Who is this Jesus?*

The priests speak to one another and they are greatly affronted. "We told Pilate to write not that he is The King of the Jews, but only that he *said* he is the King of the Jews, but Pilate only said, 'What I have written, I have written.'" And they murmur thus among themselves.

Through my haze of drugged pain, I notice that four soldiers take my garments and split them between themselves. Other soldiers take Jesus' garments, and make four parts, and give to every soldier a portion. And when they lift up his coat, one says, "Let us not rend it, for it is without seam, woven from the top throughout, but let us cast lots for it, whose it shall be."

And then, incredibly, Jesus pushes up on his feet so he can exhale and speak, and utters the second words I have heard from him. "Father, forgive them, for they know not what they do."

He forgives the *Romans*? For crucifying him? For casting lots for his clothing?

I need to exhale, too, but I wait as long as I can because the pain is so great. Finally I have to rise, and I cannot imagine doing so in order to forgive the soldiers who have crucified me.

Who is this Jesus?

And, as if in answer, another scripture comes to my pain-wracked mind, when David in his Psalms did say: *They parted my raiment among them, and for my vesture they did cast lots.*

Before my eyes, these things the soldiers do.

And the truth of it strikes me in the midst of my pain.

This Jesus *is* the King of the Jews!

He is of the House of David!

He is truly the Messiah!

And I see clearly the sin of my deeds without my excuses. The many years devoid of the Law, empty of devotion, absent of prayer. This new knowledge of my sins tortures my mind, even as the crucifixion tortures my body. I, with all my sins, hang here because of what I have done. But Jesus hangs there as a sacrifice, as the unblemished lamb.

The hope of all Israel was here, during my lifetime, and I was too hardened to take notice. And there are those more hardened than I, who would nail this very Hope to a cross!

Was it not Isaiah who said, *And He made His grave with the wicked?* And are Gestas and I not wicked? And the scripture is fulfilled which saith, *And He was numbered with the transgressors.*

I push up to exhale and sink back down to inhale. I sit back against the *sedile* at times to catch my breath and revive my strength, even as I do knowing it prolongs my agony.

They that pass by revile Jesus. They seem to ignore Gestas and me, who are guilty, but they mock Jesus, who is innocent, saying, "Thou that destroyest the temple, and buildest it in three days, save thyself, and come down from the cross."

And I look at Jesus, and again I feel the truth strike me, and this witness of the Spirit is something I have not felt for a long time.

This is the Messiah.

He could come down from the cross if He chose. Why does He not? I wonder.

The knowledge that the Messiah is here, next to me, in pain, dying as I am, causes my tears to flow.

The chief priests mock Him, saying, "He saved others; himself he cannot save."

They admit it! They admit He saved others! They know not even what they have just admitted!

Another calls out, "If he be the King of Israel, let him now come down from the cross, and we will believe him."

One throws his arms out wide in mockery. "Let Christ the King of Israel descend now from the cross, that we may see and believe."

"He trusted in God," the first chief priest mocks. "Let God deliver him now, if he will have him; for he said, I am the Son of God."

But He *is* the Son of God! I know it!

The soldiers ridicule him, as well, saying, "If thou be the King of the Jews, save thyself."

And even Gestas, another sinner like unto myself, calls out from his cross, and rails on Jesus, saying, "If thou be Christ, save thyself and us."

And I push myself up to rebuke him, ignoring the agony in my legs. "Dost not thou fear God, seeing thou art in the same condemnation?"

The exertion is too great and I have to take another breath, another excruciating movement, to finish my words. "And we indeed justly; for we receive the due reward of our deeds; but this man hath done nothing amiss . . ."

And I push up yet again, and look toward Jesus. "Lord, remember me when Thou comest into Thy kingdom."

And Jesus, the King of the Jews, Immanuel, the Son of the Living God, looks into my eyes and I am touched as though by a flame by His gaze. It burns through me as warmth floods my body, easing the agony.

Then Jesus--*the Messiah!*--pushes Himself up again to answer me--*me, a sinner!*-- and says, "Verily I say unto thee, today shall thou be with me in Paradise."

Tears run down my cheeks as a peace settles over me. *Peace!* Unbelievable that I should feel peace at the same time as my body is trying so desperately to die. But when we die, then shall I be with Jesus in Paradise! How could I *not* feel peace at that good news?

Jesus sees into my very soul and knows all about me, and still He gives this peace and forgiveness to such a one as I, who deserves the death I have received. Still He gives me life.

There is no one at my cross, nor is there any at the cross of my fellow criminal. But at the cross of Jesus are many people, many women.

One woman calls another woman by the name of Mary, and I realize from their words that this Mary is the mother of Jesus.

Isaiah's words whisper to me. *Therefore the Lord himself shall give you a sign; Behold, a virgin shall conceive, and bear a son, and shall call his name Immanuel.*

I turn my eyes again to Jesus. When he therefore sees His mother, who is weeping, and his disciple standing by, He says unto His mother, "Woman, behold thy son!"

His mother looks at the disciple beside her.
Then says Jesus to His disciple, "Behold thy mother!"

The disciple nods to show that he will take the mother of Jesus as his own. He places his arm about the mother of the Christ and comforts her and takes her to his home.

The sun continues to rise in the sky, marking my pain. Is it the sun or a fever that makes me burn? Or the pain in my nerve endings? I am on fire.

In the sixth hour, when the sun is directly overhead and brightest, burning me with its heat, suddenly it is darkened.

There is darkness over all the land.
Darkness in mid day. What is this?
Am I dying? Is this the end?
I hear women cry out in fear.

And my pain continues on unabated and thus I realize I am still among the living. I shed tears at the knowledge.

Without sight, the focus of my existence becomes my body and my pain and my fight to stay alive, to breathe out so that I may in turn breathe in.

I listen for sounds to distract me. The fear of the crowd calling to one another for reassurance. The wind blowing. The women crying.

With the sun darkened, a chill sets in. I shiver in my nakedness. The wind picks up and I shake. Each tremor adds to my pain, my everlasting agony.

The darkness is a new torment to add to the old. Fear intensifies my pain. The absence of the light, of all light, brings a sadness to my soul that no night has ever matched.

And I know for a surety that my drink contained myrrh and not hemlock, else I would be dead by now.

How will the Jews or the soldiers know when the Sabbath begins, if the darkness is already here? And what does it mean, this darkness in the mid day when there should be light?

I know not, and I push up to breathe out so that I may drag in another breath.

I fade in and out of consciousness. I have lost track of time in the darkness and pain. It seems as though many hours have passed.

Finally, in the darkness, Jesus cries with a loud voice, "*Eli, Eli, lama sabachthani?*"

My God, my God, why hast thou forsaken me? Those are the very words King David wrote generations ago. *Why art thou so far from helping me, and from the words of my roaring?*

And some of those on the ground are mistaken and say, "This man calleth for Elias."

Only after Jesus calls out does the light return.

The sun, as if it had been there all along, traveling across the sky though we could not see it, appears still high, lighting the world again in its normal manner.

It must only be about the ninth hour, so we have been in darkness only about three hours. There are three hours until the sunset and the Sabbath, and so only two more of suffering before I will be dead and taken from the cross and my body discarded like refuse.

When the light of the sun appears, Jesus pushes up and sighs, as He has not done before, and says, "I thirst."

Yet another Psalm enters my mind. *My strength is dried up like a potsherd; and my tongue cleaveth to my jaws; and thou has brought me into the dust of death.*

The dust of death. My own thirst has built until it wracks every cell of my body. And I have not lost blood as Jesus had before He was crucified. His thirst must be tremendous.

At Jesus' words--*I thirst*--straightway someone runs and takes a sponge, fills it with the pain-deadening wine and puts it on a reed, and gives Him to drink. I see it is the same Simon of Cyrene who carried His cross. I can tell from his face that Simon has eyes to see and knows who Jesus is.

The rest still mock Him. "Let him be, let us see whether Elias will come to save him."

Even after the three hours of darkness, of even the sun withholding its light in protest for what they have done, can they still not see? And would I not see if I was not here, hanging upon this cross?

Then for that reason I am glad to be here, suffering this excruciating pain, for I have seen the Christ.

I have seen the fulfilment of divine prophecy.

I have seen the Messiah and felt the peace of His forgiveness.

I would not give up this knowledge even for life itself. Even for the absence of this present agony.

When Jesus therefore receives the wine, with one last surge of strength, he once again presses His torn and bleeding feet against the nail, pushes up, takes a breath and shouts out with a loud voice, "Father, it is finished. Thy will is done."

Then Jesus says, "Father, into thy hands I commend my spirit." And, having said thus, He drops down, bows His head, and gives up the ghost.

He gives up His life!

No one takes it from Him! They could not!

And I am so alone in this moment. Oh, that I could be with him already!

And, behold, the earth quakes, and the rocks rend.

Now when the centurion, and they that are with him, watching Jesus, hear the earthquake, and that He so cried out with a loud voice, which men before they die on the cross do not do, and gave up the ghost, he glorifies God and says, "Truly this man *is* the Son of God."

And I know again that this is true.

And all the Jews, beholding the things which are done, smite their breasts with grief and possibly some with repentance.

Though my body aches and is tortured with every breath, though I struggle to live and yet yearn to die, peace comes into my heart again as I remember the words of the Christ to me, a sinner.

"Verily I say unto thee, today shall thou be with me in Paradise."

And, because God and His Son cannot lie, I know it is truth.

Then I do what I could never have imagined doing upon the cross, in the midst of my agony. I smile.

The Savior has come, and I am saved.

And soon shall I be with Him in Paradise.

Peter was grieved
because He said unto him
the third time,
'Lovest thou me?'

(John 21:17)

FEED MY SHEEP
Simon Peter

At the sea of Tiberias, I went a fishing.

With me came these others: Thomas called Didymus, Nathanael of Cana in Galilee, James and John the sons of Zebedee, and two other of Jesus' disciples. Seven of us on the ship, fishing in the moonlight, and we have caught nothing.

Through these warm hours of fishless fishing under the stars, I have had much time to think. And my thoughts have led to Jesus. Of His saying He would make us fishers of men. Of our day-to-day comradeship with the Lord. Of the miracles, the blessing of the children, the loaves and fishes.

There are things I do not want to remember, as well. The kiss of Judas the betrayer. Jesus' scourging and death. The sound of the cock crowing when I realized that I *had* denied Him thrice, just as He had foretold.

The remembrance rips at me anew. I wept that night, bitterly, for many reasons. I have not wept since, though my wife tells me I have need of it. But I will not cry. I am a stone, for so Jesus called me. The first time He met me, He said my name would be *Cephas*, which is Aramaic. Later, He called me by the Greek word, *Peter*. Both mean stone, or rock.

Yet I always thought of stone as stable and sturdy. Thus how can I be any kind of a stone? I do feel as cold as stone inside, though, even on this warm night, as I remember that I betrayed Jesus, even as Judas did. No, not as Judas. Never as Judas.

Yet I denied knowing Him. Not once, though that would have been enough to haunt my dreams. Not twice. But, with a curse and an oath, *thrice*. Like three thorns stuck in my heart, I remember.

Some say I denied knowing Jesus out of fear. But did I not, only hours earlier, draw a sword and face a great crowd armed with swords and cudgels? And did not my Lord rebuke me for so doing?

I would have fought to the death to save Him-- except He told me to sheath my sword, and asked, "Do you suppose that I cannot appeal to my Father, who would at once send to my aid more than twenty legions of angels? But how then could the scripture be fulfilled which say this must be?"

I did not fully realize, even then, that He meant to die as He had foretold. But I began to see, faintly, He was going to sacrifice Himself, to let those men take

Him and put Him to death even though He has before walked out of other situations when death threatened.

He is the Lamb of God. Did the crowd not say, "Crucify Him" at about the noon hour, which is the very hour the priests sacrifice the paschal lamb? And I could not protect Him.

Others excuse my words by claiming my Lord instructed me to deny knowing Him so that I might be safe. I would like to soothe my conscience with that thought. But if He could ask the Father to send angels to protect Himself, could He not likewise protect me? Indeed, did He not pray for us and ask that the Father would protect us?

But if any have doubts, they need only ponder this: Would the King of Truth instruct me to tell other than the truth? No. Never. Satan is the Father of All Lies. No, Christ did not command me to lie.

The fault was indeed mine. The confusion.

I could have hidden that night, as did the others, but I, impetuous as I have ever been, could not. I was drawn, even as the truth of His words grew horribly clear: In two days' time it will be Passover, and the Son of Man is to be handed over for crucifixion. We could not comprehend as we watched Him ride into Jerusalem in triumph. Did He not ride into Jerusalem on an ass to show He came in peace? Not on a horse as a conqueror.

During that horrible night, I followed at a distance. Before I had known fear, but was always spurred by my fear to action, as when I drew my sword and cut off the right ear of Malchus, the servant of the High Priest.

But with His words of rebuke, Jesus took from me my normal response. With His action--healing the servant's ear which I had smitten--He gently reminded me of His mission.

Even in going to His death, He acted in love. Was replacing the ear not the perfect example of loving thy enemies that He commanded us we must do?

If I could not fight for my Master, then what was I to do? Great despair and confusion filled me that night. My sword was sheathed. I could not fight. Neither could I hide. I was simply to watch, and that has never been my strength or my personality.

I could only follow at a distance, pulled by the same power that drew me to leave behind my fishing nets at Jesus' words at the first. I have always followed Him. But that night He would not allow me to follow where He was going. I could not.

No matter the many reasons others give for my words that night of the illegal trials, the fact remains I did deny knowing Him. And the sound of my denials still echo within my soul. *I know Him not . . . I know Him not . . . I know Him not.*

I knew only He would die, and I was not to be allowed to help. When the cock crowed and Jesus looked into my eyes, I was overcome with grief. He *would* die. And I was expected to carry on without Him, but I felt I could not.

That was when the weight of the mantle of responsibility fell with full force upon my shoulders.

I *do* know Him. I know who He is and why He came. When Jesus asked me, I told Him thus: Thou art the Christ, the Son of the living God. *This I do know.*

Yet my thoughts this starry night upon the water avail me not for I did not speak them when they mattered.

But if I had spoken them, the crowd would have taken me, as well. As we ate of the last Passover meal which we shared, Jesus said to me, 'Simon, Simon, behold, Satan hath desired to have you, that he may sift you as wheat: But I have prayed for thee, that thy faith fail not: and when thou art converted, strengthen thy brethren.'

It could not be allowed that Satan sift me as wheat, for Christ has much for me to do.

And so, though I knew I needed to stay safe but because I could not hide, I lied: *I know him not. I know not the man. I know not what thou sayest.*

A deep sadness settles upon my soul. I fear I will carry this weight of remorse always in my heart, for Jesus and I will always know what I have done--and what I have failed to do.

I check the fishing net and try to focus on my task. It is few nights that no fish enter the nets. Yet tonight the net is empty. There is nothing there--nothing but remembrance, remorse and regrets.

Finally, with a sigh, I pull myself from these thoughts, back to the moonlight flickering upon the dark waters. The water gently lapping the boat. The sway of the boat beneath me.

I try to think of happier times. When Jesus appeared to us in the closed room and showed us His hands and feet, and ate fish and honeycomb with us, and later when He showed Himself also to Thomas. When He healed the mother of my wife from her fever. The time we walked and talked together. The baskets of bread that did not empty, but rather refilled themselves. The thrill of watching Him perform many other miracles, healing as He went. How could I have denied knowing the Son of God?

Faint streaks of light on the horizon signal the coming morn. I look toward the shore and see the silhouette of a man. When I cannot make out who it is, I point him out to the others. "Know ye this man?"

They look, also, and shake their heads. "Nay, we know him not."

"Children," the man calls out to us in the Jewish manner of addressing other men, "have ye any meat?" The sound carries well over the small waves. The man's voice is vaguely familiar. Where have I heard it before?

We call out as one, "No."

The man calls out again, "Cast the net on the right side of the ship, and ye shall find."

I shrug at the others, and they shrug back. Why not? We have caught no fish. Our fishermen's instincts have this night failed us. So together we haul in the net and cast it out again on the other side of the ship--the right side. As if this is some signal to the fish, instantly they come, leaping and flying, jumping and flapping, splashing and racing to be first in the net. I watch with my mouth agape.

There are seven of us aboard, but even when we strain together to pull in the full net, we are not able to draw it for the multitude of fishes.

I have only once before seen such abundance of fish with the willingness to be caught, when a man also instructed us where to fish, and we caught so many fish our nets broke. That man—

Suddenly, John cries out, "*It is the Lord.*"

The Lord! My heart leaps within my breast for joy. I gird my fisher's coat unto me, climb onto the wooden side of the ship, cast myself into the sea and swim for shore. I do not wait for the little boat that will bring the others, for I can reach Him more quickly if I swim.

We are only two hundred cubits from shore and I cross the distance easily, using long, steady strokes and hard, regular kicks. My body has always been strong. It is my heart that grieves me of late. But in this moment I feel only joy.

My Master is here! He has come back to us once more! This is now the third time that Jesus has shown Himself to us, His disciples, after He rose from the dead.

I climb, dripping with water and with joy, from the sea and drop to my knees at the feet of my Master.

He lifts me up and pulls me into His embrace and calls me *friend*. As before, He says nothing of my denials. But I still hear their echoes.

Tears burn in my eyes and I blink them back. A stone does not weep.

The other six disciples arrive, pulling the little ship onto the shore, the net behind it in the water, full of flapping, jumping, splashing fish.

Jesus motions to us. "Bring of the fish ye have now caught."

None of us dares ask Him, Who art thou?, for we *know* He is the Lord. So the other apostles and I draw the net to land, heavy under its abundance of great fishes. We count them in amazement--a hundred and fifty and three! A catch unlike any except the one other, only this time the net is not broken.

When Jesus invites us to "Come and dine," we see a fire of coals and fish laid thereon, and bread. Jesus takes bread and fish, and gives them to us. Thus we sup with Jesus and I savor His calming presence.

After we have eaten, Jesus looks into my eyes.

I want to look away, my pain at my denial rises so strong within me, but how can any look away from the Christ? I cannot.

"Simon Peter," He says unto me gently.

My heart catches within me. Again He calls me Peter. The stone. Does He still consider me thus?

Jesus continues. "Simon, son of Jonas, lovest thou me more than these?"

"Yea, Lord," I respond, my voice choking, "Thou knowest that I love thee."

And I know He loves me, as well, for that love shines from His eyes and warms my soul.

"*Feed my lambs.*" His voice is powerful yet gentle, as if He knows I have need of reassurance.

If Christ entrusts me with this task, I will gladly do it. This time I will prove I will endure anything. I *will* be Cephas. I *will* be Peter. I *will* be the rock, steady and true. "Yea, Lord."

He continues to look at me and asks a second time, "Simon, son of Jonas, lovest thou me?"

Though His voice is soft, each word pierces me. "Yeah, Lord, thou knowest that I love thee." *I know I denied knowing Thee, but I love Thee with all my heart and soul.*

Jesus says unto me, "*Feed my ewes.*"

The others have grown quiet around us, but my focus is not on them. I cannot look from Jesus' eyes as He asks a third time, with great power, "Simon, son of Jonas, lovest thou me?"

I am sore grieved because He asks me a third time, *Lovest thou me?* Does He truly not know? Have my denials wiped away everything else good between us? My heart cries out within me of my love for Jesus. This third time His words pierce so deeply into my soul that my tears flow forth and course down my cheeks.

Finally, this stone cries. "Lord, thou knowest all things," I cry out in anguish. "Thou knowest that I love thee."

"*Feed my rams,*" comes the next gentle command. Jesus nods His approval, and continues to speak to me. "Verily, verily, I say unto thee, when thou was young, thou girdest thyself, and walketh whither thou would;

149

but when thou shalt be old, thou shalt stretch forth thy hands, and another shall gird thee, and carry thee whither thou would not."

And I know He speaks thus to signify by what death I shall glorify God. *Glorify God*? Me? One who denied His Lord?

I understand, now, that crucifixion awaits me. And I will gladly follow my Lord upon the cross, though I am unworthy to be hung as He was. Jesus knows I have never feared to follow Him, and thus I care not what men say.

As I continue to gaze into His eyes, my tears are no longer bitter, but they wash the thorns from my heart. In His eyes, I see many things. Jesus asked me thrice, and thrice I answered Him. And He asked me thrice not because He doubted my love, but because He knew I doubted myself. And I know in this instant that I can no longer listen to any echoes of what I wish I could change, for if I listen to them, I will not clearly hear His voice and thus will be unfit to do His work.

Even as before I denied Him thrice, I have now reaffirmed my love for Him thrice. And I see that these three answers have outweighed my three denials. As I have watched Jesus heal so many others, now I feel the miracle within my own heart as Jesus heals *me*. The thorns are gone, the echoes silent, the pain drained away.

When Jesus touches my shoulder, a smile breaks forth on my face. My spirit lightens. My resolve strengthens. I am forgiven. A rush of gratitude fills my heart and I am amazed anew at the healing power of Jesus' Atonement and the Father's love that knows no bounds.

I will not falter again, for any reason. If Jesus still considers me a stone, a rock, then I *will* be a stone. If He asks me to feed His sheep, then I *will* feed His sheep.

The first time He ever said unto me, "Follow me," I dropped my nets and followed Him in that very instant.

Now He says unto me, yet again, "Follow me. Feed my sheep."

And I will not falter again.

I will declare the truth to all, no matter where I find myself, even if the very legions of Rome should surround me.

I will say it unto all, as I said it before.

Jesus is the Christ, the Son of the living God.

I know it. And you may know it, as well.

And it came to pass,
while He blessed them,
He was parted from them, and
carried up into heaven.

(Luke 24:51)

YE MEN OF GALILEE
John

My heart is heavy this day. This may be the last time I see Christ for many, many years. Centuries, certainly. Millennia, perhaps.

We, the eleven remaining apostles, walk to the mount where He first ordained and appointed us, when there were yet twelve. He has asked us to meet Him there.

So I walk beside Peter, his brother Andrew, and my brother James. Philip, Bartholomew who is also called Nathanael, and Thomas Didymus who doubted no more than we when he first saw the resurrected Christ.

Levi Matthew the publican, who left the house of the collection of taxes to follow Christ. James, the son of Alpheus.

Judas, the brother of James, who is also called Lebbacus, whose surname is Thaddeus. And Simon the Zealot.

A council of eleven, brothers in Christ.

We are followed by others, believers and those who wish to believe.

The sun shines hot through the perfectly white clouds, its rays glowing in a celestial-appearing manner.

It has been forty days since His resurrection. In that time, Jesus has done many signs and miracles in our presence. If all that He has done while on the earth were recorded, I suppose even the world itself could not contain the books that should be written.

I am John, the disciple whom the Lord loveth. The disciple who, along with Peter and James, have been privy to many blessed events, among them the transfiguration.

But I alone have extra responsibility weighing upon me, for I have been honored by the Lord to watch over His mother as my own. So I know He trusts me to stay faithful at least until she passes from this life.

But I will not pass from this life. I will tarry until the Lord returns to the earth. I had no regrets when I asked Jesus if I could tarry, but I have doubts this day.

Can I endure to the end when the end is so far away?

I do not want to do as Judas did, to fall away when I have been so blessed.

I do not want to fall away as I have been shown that many in the church will do during the trials to come.

If I can perform my mission well, then I shall spread the truth on the earth for perhaps thousands of years, while my fellow apostles do their work on the other side.

But this day they walk beside me. There are eleven of us now, we men of Galilee. Judas Iscariot was not from Galilee, but from Judea, but Judas is no longer.

I know Jesus saw what Judas was before He called Him--and yet He called Him. I wonder . . . what did Jesus see of me before He called me? Will I also fail in my mission?

I try to trust in my Lord, but today I am full of doubts. I am strong now, but can I be strong forever? I do not want to let Him down.

Soon we approach the mount, the same mount upon which Jesus spoke the sermon of the Blessed Are's.

Blessed are they which are persecuted for righteousness' sake: for theirs is the kingdom of heaven.

Jesus was persecuted. And now, as we follow Jesus since His death and resurrection, we are also reviled. All Christ's disciples.

My brother James walks beside me, and I glance at him. We are the sons of Zebedee, first followers of The Baptist, and when he told us of Jesus, we then followed the Messiah with all our hearts. The Lord, Himself, called us *Boanerges--The Sons of Thunder*--for our oft misplaced zeal. James and I even wanted to call down fire from the heavens as did Elias in order to destroy Samaritan villagers who refused hospitality to our Lord, but Jesus rebuked us gently, saying, "Ye know not what manner of spirit ye are of. For the Son of Man is not come to destroy men's lives, but to save them."

I have great zeal, but can it continue thus? Will the evil one find my weakness and bring me down?

I have already proven my weakness. Was it not Peter, James and I who were closest to Jesus when He suffered for our sins in the Garden of Gethsemane? When He needed me to pray for Him, did I not sleep?

That night when He told us, "My soul is exceeding sorrowful, even unto death. Tarry ye here, and watch with me," and we heard Him pray to the Father, "Abba, all things are possible unto Thee. Take away this cup from me; nevertheless, not what I will, but what Thou wilt."

But even hearing all that, when He returned, we were asleep, and He had to ask of us, "What, could ye not watch with me one hour? Watch and pray that ye enter not into temptation."

Even when He prayed a second time, saying, "O my Father, if this cup may not pass away from me, except I drink it, Thy will be done," and we saw that He was in an agony and His sweat was as it were great drops of blood falling to the ground as He atoned for our sins, still we succumbed to sleep.

He has never mentioned my weakness to me since, but I cannot help but regret. Oh, that I had stayed awake for my Lord in His hour of need. Yet even in His agony, He gave us excuse: "The spirit indeed is willing, but the flesh is weak."

Will I become stronger because of my former weakness, as Peter has shouldered the weight of the church since he denied Christ thrice? Or will I grow weaker as the years pass and as I go through trials and persecution until I fail as did Judas?

Blessed are ye, when men shall revile you, and persecute you, and shall say all manner of evil against you falsely, for my sake. Rejoice, and be exceeding glad: for great is your reward in heaven: for so persecuted they the prophets which were before you.

As we who are left go now onto the mountain, we catch sight of our risen Lord, walking toward us.

My heart fills with love and awe. I worship Him, as do my fellow Apostles, but some other followers doubt. They doubt His body has been risen, because of the lies spread by the Sadducees and Pharisees who claim Jesus was taken from the cross while yet alive and so has not taken up his body again from death. But we know the truth of the risen, resurrected Christ.

Yet even we, the ten of us first and Thomas after, touched the wounds in His hands and His feet, and the wound in His side caused by the spear of the Roman soldier, in order to fully believe what had never been known before.

Jesus greets us, and says, "All power is given unto me in heaven and in earth."

And truly He seems to glow as with sunlight, with glory and power.

He watches as we gather around Him, and then He smiles and continues, "Go ye into all the world, and preach the gospel to every creature."

When He first appointed and ordained us, He set us apart to teach the lost sheep of the House of Israel. He is now opening His Gospel to all the earth.

157

Thus we are to take His teachings to all, Gentile and Jew, Greek and Roman, bond and free, man, woman and babe. All children of God.

Blessed are the peacemakers: for they shall be called the children of God.

"Go ye therefore," He repeats, "and teach all nations, baptizing them in the name of the Father, and of the Son, and of the Holy Ghost. He that believeth and is baptized shall be saved, but he that believeth not shall be damned."

He motions to us all, opening His arms to us who believe and have been baptized--and also those who doubt.

"And these signs shall follow them that believe: In my name shall they cast out devils; they shall speak with new tongues; they shall take up serpents. And if they drink any deadly thing, it shall not hurt them. They shall lay hands on the sick, and they shall recover."

All these things may happen to us--*to me*--in the persecution which is to come. Yet Jesus is assuring us that we will survive much evil. Assuring me I will have sufficient strength until He comes again. And I do much need this assurance, for I will be here long upon the earth.

"Teach them to observe all things whatsoever I have commanded you. And, behold, I send the promise of my Father upon you: but tarry ye in the city of Jerusalem, until ye be endued with power from on high. For John truly baptized with water; but ye shall be baptized with the Holy Ghost not many days hence."

158

He beckons us, the same Messiah whom we have harkened after since He first said unto us, *"Follow me."* That same moment when we could do nothing save lay aside our nets and became fishers of men. How could we not follow the Messiah when we recognized Him?

That moment when He told us, "From henceforth thou shalt take men alive," fulfilling the prediction through Jeremiah, that in reaching scattered Israel, He would send for many fishers, and they would fish them.

I would follow Jesus to the ends of the earth and beyond. Today He leads us the easy walking distance to Bethany.

He stops and moves to Peter and speaks to Him alone. Then He moves to Andrew. He steps to each of us in turn, His eleven men of Galilee who have followed Him thus far.

When He reaches me, and looks into my eyes and places His hand upon my shoulder, I am shaken with the love I feel for my Savior and for the love that shines forth from His eyes to me.

If He were to tell me once again, *"Follow me,"* I would follow Him again, no matter what end we may all come to.

Jesus blesses me and I feel my body changed. I feel myself renewed and strengthened. I feel my body is no longer one of the trials I will face.

Have I been changed so that I might live and not die as the others? In order that the evil one might not have power over me? Jesus nods His head in answer to my unspoken questions.

I sense He is saying goodbye in this moment, though He uses other words, and I feel the loss of His presence already.

Too soon, He leaves me and moves on to Philip, to Andrew, and to each of the others, all men of good hearts.

Blessed are all the pure in heart: for they shall see God.

We have seen and walked with the Son of God and, knowing the Son, we know the Father.

We stand before Jesus now, surrounded by other followers. One Apostle asks, "Lord, wilt thou at this time restore again the kingdom to Israel?"

Jesus answers, "It is not for you to know the times or the seasons, which the Father hath put in His own power. But ye shall receive power, after that the Holy Ghost is come upon you: and ye shall be witnesses unto me both in Jerusalem, and in all Judea, and in Samaria, and unto the uttermost part of the earth."

Jesus lifts up His hands, and blesses us.

Blessed are the merciful: for they shall obtain mercy.

"And, lo, I am with you always, unto the end of the world. Amen."

And it comes to pass, while He blesses us, His feet lift from off the ground!

I gasp, as do the others.

We step back in amazement.

Jesus is lifted further from the ground, up into the air, above the olive trees, among the flying birds.

Up toward the clouds.

His hands are still open wide, as if waiting to receive us to Him.

I worship Him, along with the others, as we watch Him rise into the sky. He ascends into the clear blue sky toward the clouds.

I watch in amazement. The brilliance that comes from Him lights the sky even more than the sun, as it did when He was transfigured.

The light of The Son.

Chills run along my limbs and make me tremble in my core.

In the clouds I see a hint of angels.

The clouds receive Him from our sight, and still we watch steadfastly, waiting to catch another glimpse of the man who was more than a man who walked among us.

My heart is in awe. Truly Jesus is the Son of God, the Messiah. How could He be anyone but?

As I gaze upward still, two personages appear, clothed in white. One says to us, "Ye men of Galilee, why stand ye gazing up into heaven? This same Jesus, which is taken up from you into heaven, shall so come in like manner as ye have seen Him go into heaven."

And thus Jesus goes from this earth, and I see clearly that His kingdom is not of this earth, but of heaven, to which He has returned in glory.

We will go now to Jerusalem to await the promise of the Father, the gift of the Holy Ghost, before we go forth to all the nations.

161

Blessed are they which do hunger and thirst after righteousness: for they shall be filled.

We eleven men of Galilee will do as Jesus instructed and take His words to all the children of God. And we will write enough of what Jesus did and said to help them believe that Jesus is the Christ, the Son of God, and that, believing, they might have life through His name.

The sacred name of Jesus, the very Christ. The very Jehovah whose name we do not say out of reverence and so I say it not aloud even now.

Christ rose in resurrection.

Now Christ has risen in His glory.

And I look forward to the time when I shall see Him return again in this same glory.

Would that I could be here upon this same Mount, but no man will know the time of His coming.

I feel most blessed.

Blessed are we for the Messiah has come--and will come yet again in glory.

Let us have life through His holy name.

This is the record of the disciple which testifieth of these things, and writes these things. And we know that his testimony is true.

Amen.

And Amen.

AUTHOR'S NOTE

Though I have tried to keep the accounts as scripturally accurate as possible, on occasion I have taken license with small details.

For example, in the story of the wise man, though the number of wise men is not stated in the scriptural account, I have stayed with the traditional number of three and even used their traditional names.

In the story of the thief upon the cross, Simon of Cyrene was indeed called out of the crowd to carry Jesus' cross, but there is no mention of him being the one who took the vinegar to Jesus.

In the second story about Peter (I could have done an entire book on Peter alone!), I used the wording as found in the Italian translation of the New Testament, where the Lord refers to three distinct type of sheep: lambs, ewes, and rams. I very much like that image.

It's been a wonderful experience for me to write this book, and I hope an enjoyable experience for you to travel the ancient roads of the Holy Land with the Savior.

If you have enjoyed reading *Men Who Knew The Mortal Messiah*, I'd love to hear from you. Get on my website (heatherhorrocks.com) and send me an email.

And now, I'd like to present the story of Esther, which I love. It's from the next book in the series. And one day I *do* plan to write an entire book about Esther.

EXCERPT

WOMEN WHO KNEW
The Pre-Mortal Messiah

Stories of Twelve
Old Testament Women
of Faith

Available Soon

And Haman said unto King Ahasuerus,

'There is a certain people scattered abroad
and dispersed among the people
in all the provinces of thy kingdom;
and their laws are diverse from all people;
neither keep they the king's laws;
therefore it is not for the king's profit
to suffer them. If it please the king,
let it be written that they may be destroyed:
and I will pay ten thousand talents of silver
to the hands of those
that have the charge of the business,
to bring it into the king's treasuries.'

And the king took the ring from his hand,
and gave it unto Haman.

(Esther 3:8-10)

FOR SUCH A TIME AS THIS

Esther

(About 470 B.C.)

Hatach, the chamberlain whom King Ahasuerus has appointed to attend me, brings me word that Mordecai wears sackcloth and ashes, as if in grief. He mourns at the gates of Shushan, the winter capitol of the land of Persia and Media.

I marvel as to what has occurred to bring my cousin, Mordecai, who raised me from a child after my parents died, to such grief. I send clothing to him, but my servants return soon and say he refuses to wear it.

I give Hatach a commandment to Mordecai, to know the cause of the sackcloth. As I wait for him to return, I try not to worry, but how can I not?

As long as I have known Mordecai, since he adopted me and became my father, he has been my steady rock. He would not grieve without a cause.

I have my own grief, that my husband has not called me to him for thirty days. In the House of Women, thirty days is a lifetime. I know not why, for we had no argument. There was no warning. I know only that the man Haman, who has been raised up second only to the king, has caught his ear and whispers the names of his other women as they drink wine late into the night.

I busy myself while I wait, my stomach clenched with fear.

When Hatach returns, there are wrinkles of concern on his forehead. "Queen Esther," he reports, "Mordecai told me a fantastic tale. Haman cast lots for many days to find an auspicious day, the thirteenth day of the twelfth month, which is the month of Adar. Then he went to the king and spun a tale of a people causing mischief in the kingdom. Haman asked the king if he might be allowed to put these people to death, and vowed to pay ten thousand talents into the treasury." Hatach shakes his head in disbelief.

"Ten thousand talents?" The enormous fortune represented by this bribe proves the rumors of Haman's wealth. If it is true, the payment would be more than half the income of the entire Persian Empire for one year. It is an incredible sum. "But what people could cause so much mischief to be worth such a princely sum?"

Hatach leans closer and lowers his voice. "Mordecai says that on the auspicious day chosen, the Jews will be put to death."

The Jews? The Jews are *my* people.

My Hebrew name, the one by which I was called in Mordecai's home, was Hadassah, meaning *myrtle*, a flower. When I went into the House of Women, I was given a new Persian name, Esther, befitting my new life as concubine of the king. And the king raised up this *star* to become his queen.

This is a great honor, to be queen of this empire ruled by my husband, King Ahasuerus, which extends from India even unto Ethiopia, over an hundred and seven and twenty provinces. Though the king does not know this, in one of these provinces lies the homeland of my people.

When I went into the House of Women, Mordecai charged me not to reveal my kinship or my people, and I did as my father commanded. Thus the king, my husband, knew not my kindred when the evil Haman came to him with his plan to destroy us all, man, woman, and babe.

The Jews have lived peaceably in Persia for many years, from the time Cyrus the Great King freed my people from their captivity by the Babylonians. He allowed us freedom to go back to our homeland and rebuild our temple. At that time, 50,000 Jews returned to Jerusalem, though many, among them my ancestors, decided to remain and thus are still scattered throughout the empire.

This same Cyrus the Great King is the noble lineage from which my husband springs. Cyrus is the great-great-grandfather to my King Ahasuerus, who has agreed to allow others to put my people to death.

I grow dizzy.

Hatach and one of my maidens assist me into a chair. "Are you well, my queen?"

I nod and wave my hand. My mouth is dry as I ask, "And what mischief have these Jews caused?"

He hesitates but for a moment. "I have heard of none save Mordecai's refusal to bow to Haman at the gate."

"Then it is revenge and pride for which the Jews will die."

"Yes." Hatach waits for my next command, holding a scroll in his hands.

But I am too stunned to give a command, too shocked to ask what new horror the scroll might contain.

I am astounded. Hatach would kill hundreds of thousands to bring one man to his knees? He would slaughter an entire people to assuage his wounded pride? I cannot comprehend the evil.

Thus because of one man's pride and desire for revenge, my people will cease to exist on the thirteenth day of the twelfth month, which is the month of Adar.

Would Haman still have dared to commit this unthinkable evil if he knew of my kinship? He has done everything else to shake me from the king's affections. Does he now seek only Mordecai's death and those of his people--or has he learned that by this action he will also be rid of the queen he desires to displace?

I shake my head. If the king knew of my kindred now, surely he would reverse the edict. But he does not call for me, so how will he learn? Who will tell him? This is a nightmare. "Surely this cannot be true."

Hatach hands me the scroll. A copy of the royal decree. I take the scroll and scan the writing. When my eyes reach the bottom, I feel faint once more. "It is sealed with the king's ring!"

If only the king, my husband, had not allowed Haman to seal the decree. Woe unto my people. A decree sealed with the king's ring has the seal of finality, of forever, of futility. It cannot be undone. With that seal even the king, himself, cannot reverse what he has ordered. Whatever decree is thus signed by the king and his lords together cannot be changed, but remains unalterable. And Haman signed with the king's ring.

This is the custom of the Persians, and has been for many generations. It is this same custom that caused me to become queen, for Queen Vashti would not come when bidden to display her beauty immodestly before the king and his visitors, all drunken with wine, and for this she was put aside. I know the king would have taken her up again, if the seal of the ring and signature of the lords had not been used in the sending away.

Now I am queen in Vashti's place.

The seal of the ring will be the undoing of both the queens of Ahasuerus.

"There is more, my queen." Hatach looked concerned.

"What is it?" I ask, afraid. What else?

"Mordecai told me to give you a charge." He glanced at me as if to see how I would react to a man at the gate giving the queen a command. "He said for you to go in unto the king, to make supplication unto him in behalf of your people."

So Hatach now knows I am a Jew. But I can barely be concerned about that, when I have so much more to fear. There is a law that has been in place since

Deioces, king of the Medes, overcame the rule of the Assyrians two hundred years ago. No one can come into the king's chambers uninvited or they risk death. I cannot do as Mordecai asks or I may die and thus be of no help to my people.

Since Mordecai, himself, has revealed my kinship, I am free to ask thus: "I must speak with Mordecai."

"I will arrange it."

And thus Hatach brings Mordecai to the chambers where I can speak with him face to face.

It is a shock to see Mordecai dressed in ashes and sackcloth and his face gaunt, but now I know the cause. I explain to him my fear and remind him of the law. "All the king's servants and the people of the king's provinces do know that whosoever, whether man or woman, shall come unto the king into the inner court, who is not called, there is one law of his to put him to death, except such to whom the king shall hold out the golden scepter, that he may live."

Even if I was not so obviously in disfavor with the king, I would never have dared to enter his throne room uninvited. But now? I dare not. His queens are not immune to his decisions. Vashti has been banished.

And in my fear, a thought comes to me. Vashti was put aside because she came not when the king bid her come--and I will be put to death because I go when the king has *not* called me.

"You must overcome your fear, my daughter."

172

But I cannot. I have never heard of any going into the king's presence uninvited, save for the ones who wear the sash of royal purple, as do the king's seven princes, who are his advisers, and the evil Haman. None else in the kingdom dares enter, or the King would decide their fate with his golden scepter. At the King's whim, they will live--or hang upon a sharp stick and die a horribly painful death.

I close my eyes and draw in a deep breath. I am surprised Mordecai has not already heard. When I open them, I share my shame with Mordecai. "I have not been called to come in unto the king these thirty days."

How can I possibly know if after thirty days the king will look upon me with favor if I enter his throne room unbidden? I have heard rumors of the flattering words Haman has used to remind the king of his other women, and have seen other concubines leave the House of Women, as they choose to pass close by my courts so I may more easily see them. And I have heard rumors of the virgins also being called to the king. None has been called twice, but so many others going to the king does not bode well for the king's reaction to me.

Mordecai takes my hand and commands me, saying, "Think not with thyself that thou shalt escape in the king's house, more than all the Jews. For if thou altogether holdest thy peace at this time, then shall there enlargement and deliverance arise to the Jews from another place; but thou and thy father's house shall be destroyed."

He touches my cheek gently. "And who knoweth whether thou art come to the kingdom for such a time as this?"

His soft-spoken words strike at my heart and conscience, despite my fear, even intensifying my fear. I know his words are true as he speaks them, for chills run along my limbs. Mordecai has always spoken truth to me, from the time I was a small child and he told me my parents had died and he would care for me. My Lord has also always spoken truth to me, and I recognize these chills in my limbs as one of His voices.

Thus I have no choice. If I go in uninvited to the king, I may die--but I also may live. If I do not go in, I will die of a surety on the thirteenth day of Adar. My kindred will become known to all. It will be a relief to have it known. And my heart swells at the thought of my people and what I can do for them.

I take another deep breath. The time for faintness has passed. "I will do as you instruct, despite my great fear. Since I must appeal to my husband, who does not send for me, I must needs go to him. And, because I go unbidden, I need the prayers and fasting of my people. I need the Lord's assistance in accomplishing such a frightening thing, and to soften the king's heart toward me."

I pause as I ponder what must needs come next and listen to a whispering of the spirit. I tell Mordecai. "Go, gather together all the Jews that are present in Shushan. Fast ye for me, and neither eat nor drink three days, night or day. I also and my maidens will fast likewise. And so will I go in unto the king, which is not according to the law. And if I perish, I perish."

But I do not wish to perish.

As Mordecai departs to do my bidding, I begin my fast and pray for inspiration.

On the second day of our fast, the Lord shows a complex plan to my mind. It is perfect. I have been at court and in the women's chambers long enough to have learned the ways of intrigue--and the ways of my king. If I go into his inner courts uncalled, I must do so with my head held high and an inviting smile upon my lips. That is my best chance of survival, for the king is fascinated when others around him are not intimidated, though he would not admit it.

If he allows me to live, then will I invite him to a banquet. And I will also invite Haman--an exclusive banquet and invitation that will make Haman, proud peacock that he is, swell with pride. And I invite the enemy of my people because otherwise he may advise the king not to return to my banquets and also because I want him present when I accuse him before the king.

At the first banquet, I plan to again avoid any direct request. I will further intrigue the king by inviting them both again to a second banquet on the following day. If all goes well at the second banquet, I will then reveal only that someone has ordered my destruction and that of my people. Only when the king asks who has done such a thing shall I reveal that the attacker of the queen and her people is Haman.

And then I must hope that the king will stand by his second queen, as he did not with his first.

If the king allows me to live by holding out his golden scepter toward me, I will have simply passed the first hardship. Then I must put into play the rest of my plan.

The days of fasting pass more slowly than any I have ever lived, even those when I was first taken into the House of Women. It has now been three days and three nights since I have partaken of food or water. During this time I have worn my clothes of mourning. I cling to the words of Mordecai, the powerful ones that give me the courage I sorely need to do what I must.

And who knoweth whether I have come to the kingdom for such a time as this?

What else can I think? Any other thoughts lead only to despair, and I cannot afford despair or all is lost-- not only for me, but for my people. So I replace fearful thoughts with prayer.

But the time for prayer is nearly over, as is the time for fasting. Now is the time for faith through deeds.

I instruct my maidens, who are as weak with hunger as am I, and the king's chamberlains to finish setting up the banquet in my outer courts. I can smell the food already being prepared and it tortures me.

Oh, my Lord, be with me this day and on the morrow, for I cannot do this alone. Do not let me falter or show my fear. Let the king remember his love for me. Let me intrigue my husband, the king.

176

My husband, who has not called me to him for thirty days. Never before has it been so long. Why did this crisis have to come now, when I am in his disfavor and not his thoughts?

I shudder with my fear and pray again to my Lord for strength to face my test. To accept my death, if need be.

For even if I succeed in convincing the king to spare my life this day, to support my cause and put Haman to death, the truth remains that the king cannot reverse his own royal decree. Any in the kingdom on the thirteenth day of Adar may kill any Jew.

Thus I am thankful for the thoughts the Lord has placed into my head. The king cannot reverse the decree, but I must convince him to issue a second order giving the Jews permission to defend themselves on that same day. Simply by issuing the second order, the king will show that he favors the Jews, and cause others to hesitate to act upon the first decree.

It is our only hope as a people. I see that now. I see why I was honored to be in this position at this time.

But why do I worry now about what only comes later? I still have to go into the king's chamber and face the possibility of my early death there. I must prepare now for *that* moment, not for any that may follow. And I cannot linger longer or I will lose what courage I have gained by fasting.

It is time.

I chew a sprig of mint to freshen my breath, for sour breath from fasting will not help my cause.

I kneel with my three maidens, who have also fasted with me. They are not Jewish, but are good women. We pray to my Lord, and they weep as they prepare me to go as a queen to my king.

Uninvited, the word comes unbidden to my mind. I reply to myself, *"For such a time as this."*

I remove my clothes of mourning. My maidens help me bathe, and perfume me as the king prefers. Two of my maidens are also bathed and dressed and given mint to chew, also, as they will attend me.

They dress me in my royal apparel. They kohl my eyes and style my hair, place gems upon my fingers and ears and around my throat and wrist.

Last of all, they place the headdress crown of a Persian queen upon my head, which rests as heavily upon my brow as does the responsibility for the lives of my people upon my heart.

The words of Mordecai again fill my mind. *And who knoweth whether thou art come to the kingdom for such a time as this?*

For such a time as this.

A time as this.

As this.

The time has come.

I push down the fear that threatens to overwhelm me. I look into the glass one last time to check my reflection there. Though my ladies exclaim of my great beauty, to myself I look pale, whether more from fear or fasting I know not.

I step into the hallway and meet the chief eunuch, Feroz, who will accompany me. He has been a friend and I can tell he is concerned.

But from this moment forth, I am Queen, and will show my fear to no one. I can no longer afford to even *feel* my fear.

As I walk the halls of the House of Women, leave its confines, and then into the King's House, a small crowd of servants and officials trail after. I can hear their astonished murmuring. They know the king has not called me, for information such as that is common knowledge in the court.

Though I feel warmth flood my cheeks, I hold my head high and hope the color improves my beauty.

Two of my faithful maidens attend me, as befits a queen. One walks beside me, and I touch her arm, as if for support. Another follows to hold the train of my royal apparel.

Light-headed, I smile and greet the Minister of Finance. Flustered, he bows deeply. I greet others who are of exalted rank and none other, for today I must be Queen Esther and not simply Esther, who was once Hadassah. It is but a role I play, and soon I will know how well I have played it.

I feel as though I am walking toward a lion's den. The lion is an ancient symbol of power and royalty in Persia. It is as though I walk in Daniel's footsteps, that same Daniel who was thrown into the lion's den in Babylon by King Darius the Mede, who was the governor of Babylon under Cyrus the Great King of

Persia. I take heart in knowing that even lions with great claws and teeth were stopped from harming Daniel. I pray I will be likewise protected from harm.

As we approach the king's chambers, I slow my steps, and turn to Feroz. "Thank you, old friend."

His eyes flutter with emotion, but he also shows great dignity. "My queen, may Ahura Mazda bless you in your quest."

He invokes the Persian god of light, but I know Who will be in the throne room with me. "Yes. May the Lord indeed bless me."

For such a time as this have I come.

I am come.

I wish I could leave my maidens outside the doors, but they must come with me as I play queen. If my fate is death, so will it be for them.

Thus I enter the lion's den trailing two whose lives depend upon mine, and we three risk all for the hundreds of thousands of my people who will die if we dare not enter.

Before I can run, I take a deep breath, turn to the door and command the guards, who quickly pull open the large doors for me.

My husband sits upon his royal throne, his hand on the golden scepter as his words are written into the public records.

Haman is absent, but the seven princes of the kingdom who act as the king's advisers are there. I know them all well. Admatha, Carshena, Marsena,

Memucan, Meres, Shethar, Tarshish. Men jealous of the influence a queen might exert upon her king. They all wear their royal purple sashes. Only the king's servants and the guards posted along the walls are clothed without them. I am fully dressed, but without a purple sash I might as well be unclothed for the stir my appearance causes.

Unclothed as the King in his drunkenness wanted Vashti to come, and she would not.

Where before they all spoke and moved, now they stop, grow silent, and stare at me, amazed that any would stray into the king's chambers and risk death.

For such a time as this.

The king is dressed in his royal robes of state, woven with gold threads and precious stones. His crown rests more easily upon his head than my crown upon mine.

I catch his eye and smile warmly, as if I fear not.

Taking a deep breath of prayer, I whisper to my maiden to have courage. Her arm is trembling so that I fear the king will see. I grasp her arm more tightly to steady her.

I walk toward the king as though he will be glad to see me. "My king," I say, and I am pleased to hear that my voice does not fail me in my fear.

Some might bow, including my maidens, but I will go to him proudly and regally, as the queen of all Persia and Media and someone he will admire for her bravery. For he does admire courage.

As I walk, I smile to him invitingly, with a promise. I will him to remember our love for each other, to remember that I am his beloved queen, to remember that he does not want to lose yet another. All the things I have prayed for three days.

My hearts pounds within my breast yet I smile warmly.

I watch for the slightest signal from King Ahasuerus of what he will do. His eyes widen in surprise. He tilts his head, obviously intrigued, but he does not smile or give any other indication of my fate.

Finally, the king lifts his scepter. Which way will he hold it? Toward me or away from me? Do I live or die?

In this moment, I force myself to lift my chin. If I die, I die. *For such a time as this.*

The king's lips curve upward. He is pleased with my courage, I hope.

He holds out the golden scepter toward me!

Relief floods through me, and I hide this relief as much as before I hid my fear, for I must keep the king intrigued. My life, and also that of all my people, still remains dangling in the balance.

My maid sags in her relief. I draw near to the king and touch the top of the scepter. His lips curve up in a smile.

Then says the king unto me, "What wilt thou, Queen Esther? And what is thy request? It shall be even given thee to the half of the kingdom."

The king exaggerates what he is willing to give me. Even though I ask only one thing, I know I cannot answer directly, or he will lose interest.

The spirit whispers to me again that I need more time. Haman's power over him is still too strong, thus I need time to have the king feel of my loving influence, to have him turn his heart back to me, before I make my request. "If it seem good unto the king, let the king and Haman come this day unto the banquet that I have prepared for him."

I can tell I have piqued the king's interest. When he raises one eyebrow, I can almost read his thoughts: *She risked death to invite me to a banquet?* The corners of his mouth curve in pleasure at the thought. Then the king commands his servants, saying, "Cause Haman to make haste, that he may do as Esther hath said."

I tell the king I will await him and Haman and go to make sure the preparations are complete.

I return to my chambers on trembling legs. More open-mouthed and wide-eyed people--officials and servants alike--line the way and watch my progress in silence. I hold my head high. The eunuch Feroz walks proudly at my side.

When we reach my chambers, I turn to him again.

He smiles broadly. "Our gods are indeed powerful."

I cannot help but smile back at him. "Yes. I thank you for your prayers this day."

He looks pleased, and then grows concerned. He knows of our three-day fast. "May I bring tea to restore your strength, my queen, and that of your ladies?"

Though I will not end my fast yet, it is a kind gesture. Hungry and tired to my bones, I say, "That would be most kind."

Once again inside my courts, I hug my two brave maidens, who are still shaking. I greet my other maidens and chamberlains and announce that the king and Haman draw near.

For such a time as this.

There is still much to do, but if the Lord has protected me thus far to save His people, He will continue to keep me safe. At that thought, a great peace envelopes me. The Lord *will* protect me further.

I must be still wise in the ways of the court, but He will continue to guide me.

I draw in a deep breath. I have taken the first--and most frightening--step, into the very lion's den. The Lord has indeed given me strength beyond my own and protected me, as He did Daniel, from harm.

Thank you, Lord. Blessed be thy name.

I am grateful to Mordecai for teaching me the ways of the Lord. I look forward to meeting with Mordecai, to see the approval in his eyes at what I have done, and to ask for his wisdom in the remainder of my plan.

But for now, I listen for the sounds that will announce that King Ahasuerus and Haman approach. I will not break my fast until they have feasted and gone, for I still have need of its power. The crisis has not yet passed.

Again I feel the reassuring peace within my heart.

The king and Haman are here.

I am so thankful my Lord was here before them.

The Lord did continue to guide and protect Esther, and the plan revealed to her during her fast did happen according to her hopes.

The King did as Esther asked and issued a second decree stating that the Jews might defend themselves on that day.
Haman and his ten sons were put to death.
Esther was given the house of Haman, and Mordecai was given the King's ring and raised second only to the King.

The Jews still celebrate their deliverance as the festival of Purim each year, when the story of Esther's courage in risking her life for her Jewish people is read from the scrolls.

And in the verbal Hebrew traditions, the story is told of a descendant of Esther who travels to Jerusalem, converts, marries a Jewish princess and has a child--
a little girl named Mary,
who gives birth to the Messiah.

BIBLIOGRAPHY

JAMES E. TALMAGE, *Jesus The Christ*. Salt Lake City, Utah: Deseret Book Company, 1973.

HARRY EMERSON FOSDICK, *The Man From Nazareth*. New York: Harper and Brothers, 1949.

The New English Bible with the Apocrypha – Oxford Study Edition, New York, Oxford University Press, Inc., 1976.

The Holy Bible - Authorized King James Edition. Salt Lake City, Utah: The Church of Jesus Christ of Latter-Day Saints, 1979.

SHERRILYN KENYON (WITH HAL BLYTHE AND CHARLIE SWEET), *Character-Naming Sourcebook*. Cincinnati, Ohio: Writer's Digest Books, 1994.

PHILIP YANCEY, *Where Is God When It Hurts?* Grand Rapids, Michigan: The Zondervan Corporation, 1977.

Jesus and His Times. Pleasantville, N.Y.: The Reader's Digest Association, Inc., 1987.

The Bible Through The Ages. Pleasantville, N.Y./ Montreal: The Reader's Digest Association, Inc., 1996.

Great People of the Bible and How They Lived. Pleasantville, N.Y./ Montreal/ London/ Sydney: The Reader's Digest Association, Inc., 1974.

Who's Who in the Bible. Pleasantville, N.Y./ Montreal: The Reader's Digest Association, Inc., 1994.

BASED ON LECTURES BY LYDIA MOUNTFORD (Stenographically Recorded), *Jesus In His Homeland*. Pioneer Press.

THOMAS M. MUMFORD, *Horizontal Harmony of the Four Gospels in Parallel Columns*. Salt Lake City: Deseret Book Company, 1976.

STEVEN J. HITE & JULIE M. HITE, *The New Testament With The Joseph Smith Translation*. Orem, Utah: The Veritas Group, 1989.

LIST OF COMBINED
WOMEN AND MEN STORIES

For those of you who would like to read the stories from both *Women Who Knew* and *Men Who Knew The Mortal Messiah* chronologically, I've included this list. The Men's stories are marked with an asterisk.

To Prepare The Way - Elisabeth
The Miracle - Christ's Mother, Mary
Behold The Lamb of God - Anna the Prophetess
Child of the Star - Wise Man
A Father's Footprints - Joseph

Take These Things Hence - Dove Seller
Living Water - Samaritan Woman at Jacob's Well
Take Up Thy Bed - Man Sick of a Palsy
Arise - Widow Whose Son is Raised
Washed Clean - Woman Who Washes Feet

*Legion - Man From Whom Jesus Casts Spirits
The Healing Touch - Woman Who Touches Hem
*A Little Faith - Peter Walks with Christ
Crumbs From The Master's Table - Gentile Woman
*A Father's Plea - Man Whose Faith Falters

In The Very Act - Adulteress
*Eyes To See - Blind Man Healed on the Sabbath
The Good Part - Martha
*This Stranger - Leper Who Gives Thanks
*Thirty Pieces of Silver - Judas Iscariot

A New God - Pilate's Wife, Procula
*It Is Finished - Thief on the Cross
He Is Risen! - Mary Magdalene
*Feed My Sheep - Simon Peter
*Ye Men of Galilee - John

(Bonus Story: For This Reason Have I Come)

ABOUT THE AUTHOR

Heather Horrocks traveled the globe for seventeen years with her oilman father Reid Hullinger, mother Loya Benson, and sisters, Skye and September. They moved from South America (where Skye was born) to the Middle East and back again, with shorter jaunts to other countries tossed in just for fun.

Though she never lived in the Holy Land, she did visit as a tourist. She also attended junior high and high school on both sides of the Arabian/Persian Gulf (depending on whether she was living in Kuwait or Iran at the time she received her mail).

After returning to the United States--*There's no place like home!*--she raised her large family and started writing seriously.

She lives with her knight in shining armor (Mark) in Utah with the last two children still at home.

In her books, Heather shares the message of Jesus, His love, the truths He taught, and the healing power of His Atonement. She is pleased to add *Men Who Knew The Mortal Messiah* to *Women Who Knew*, and is excited to continue the series by traveling back further in time to the Old Testament next, writing about women in the lineage of Christ.

Word Garden 🌻 Press

"Where Good Books Are Always Blossoming"

P.O. Box 27208
Salt Lake City, Utah 84127-0208

Visit our web page
(www.WomenWhoKnew.com)
to sign up for Heather's newsletter.

Upcoming Releases

A Visit With Three Women Who Knew
(Musical Program)

You Just Turned 8: The Baptism Book

Women Who Knew The Pre-Mortal Messiah

ORDERING INFO

Find *Men Who Knew The Mortal Messiah*
and *Women Who Knew the Mortal Messiah*
in bookstores.

If your local bookstore does not carry them,
they may order copies for you by placing a
wholesale order with Deseret Book
Distribution (1-800-453-3876).
Men Who Knew The Mortal Messiah
ISBN 0-9748098-1-0
Women Who Knew the Mortal Messiah
ISBN 0-9748098-0-2

You may also purchase copies **online** at
DeseretBook.com, Amazon.com and BN.com.
While there, take a moment to read the
great five-star reviews.

For personalized autographed gift copies,
visit my website,
www.HeatherHorrocks.com.